What others are saying

Brian Connolly's *Awakened* is a powerful challenge to the present description of discipleship. It is a needed call to New Testament quality consecration. Brian's writing builds faith and understanding about what Christianity should look like, which is often quite different from what we see around us. I encourage you to buy and read *Awakened*.

—Dr. Randy Clark
Founder and President of Global Awakening
and the Apostolic Network of Global Awakening
Mechanicsburg, PA.

I have had the privilege on a number of occasions of receiving wonderful revelation from the teaching ministry of Brian Connolly. Brian's honesty, humility, and passion for Jesus shine through as he opens the Word of God. This book is remarkable in that it reads just like Brian sounds when he teaches. This is Brian's voice, his message, and his conviction as a pastor and as a man of God. You will find yourself (as I did) saying, "Yes!" or "That is so true!" under your breath as you read Brian's story of desperation and transformation under the power of the Spirit. You will never be the same.

—Mike Hutchings, Th.D.
Director of the Global School of Supernatural
Ministry and Christian Healing Certification Program
Global Awakening
Mechanicsburg, PA

As I read *Awakened*, I experienced the Holy Spirit testify with my spirit that I am a son! This kingdom work has the spirit of "sonship" all over it. Brian has loaded this book with Scriptures that declare boldly the gospel of the kingdom. As you read you will be encouraged, challenged, convicted, and above all else, transformed as Brian walks the reader through what growing closer to Jesus and glorifying God looks like practically.

—Bryan Schwartz
Pastor, Renovation Church
Former NFL Linebacker, Jacksonville Jaguars
Lafayette, CO

Brian Connolly has written an amazing book filled with truth, love, and revelation that is sure to bring freedom to the body of Christ. I believe that the words you are about to read will not only challenge you but they will initiate change in your life. My friend Brian does not only share amazing truth on the pages of this book but he courageously shares the lessons he has learned throughout his life and ministry with us. As I read *Awakened*, I was deeply moved and found myself completely overwhelmed by the mercy and love of God. I highly recommend this book as I believe it is a "now" word for the body of Christ that is sure to bring healing and change to the people who read it!

—David Wagner
Father's Heart Ministries
Pensacola, Florida

The thing that I admire most about Brian in the fifteen years that I have known him is his personal devotion to God. To see a man take prayer as seriously as he does is something to behold. The fact that Brian lets us in on any insight into what he has discovered in those times with God is precious to me and I am sure you will find it just as rewarding as well. The lines that are written in this book were wrestled down from God Himself over the course of two years and I was an eyewitness of those matches. Brian is the real deal. I hope this book spurs you deeper into devotion to God as it has done for me.

—Rev. Adam Bower
Senior Pastor
Praise Community Church
York, PA

Do you have dissatisfaction with common Christianity? Are you unfulfilled by the same old same old? The one thing burning in the author's heart is echoed in the pages of this book, living wholly devoted to our King Jesus. In *Awakened*, Brian exposes his own frustration with passive Christianity and his personal desire to live out the gospel at any cost. His hunger is contagious, imparting a new zeal for an authentic gospel. The impact of revealing Jesus in word and deed will surely light fires and change nations. This book will draw you in, encourage you and bring you further revelation of the One who has taken hold of Brian and those like him.

—Mike Van't Hul
Codirector
Loaves and Fishes International
Fuzhou, Fujian, China

Brian is a great and trusted friend of ours, and I was so excited when he told me that he was writing a second book. His first book, *First Dance*, was a journey of intimacy with Jesus. After reading his second book, *Awakened*, I believe it is the perfect follow-up to his first book because it reveals the fruit that comes from that intimacy. In looking at three examples of women in the Bible, Brian beautifully unpacked their stories and opens the door for the reader to apply the principles to their own lives. Our ministry is one to the women and children caught in sex trades and abuse and we are daily seeing the very redemption and fruit that Brian shares in this book. I cried tears of joy as he taught on the story of the woman caught in adultery and pictured our girls' faces as I read. As with his first book, there is a beautiful balance of spiritual depth and practical application and I often found myself saying, "That makes so much sense," which is always the sign of a good book in my opinion. As you read *Awakened*, you will be drawn into a deeper intimacy with the Father and empowered by His love to live a fruitful life hand in hand with Him.

—Nic Billman
Cofounder and Codirector
Shores of Grace
Recife, Brazil

AWAKENED

AWAKENED

*Coming Awake
and Coming Alive
Through the
Beauty of the Gospel*

Brian Connolly

TATE PUBLISHING
AND ENTERPRISES, LLC

Scripture quotations taken from the New American Standard Bible®, Copyright © 1960, 1962, 1963, 1968, 1971, 1972, 1973, 1975, 1977, 1995 by The Lockman Foundation. Used by permission.

This book is designed to provide accurate and authoritative information with regard to the subject matter covered. This information is given with the understanding that neither the author nor Tate Publishing, LLC is engaged in rendering legal, professional advice. Since the details of your situation are fact dependent, you should additionally seek the services of a competent professional.

The opinions expressed by the author are not necessarily those of Tate Publishing, LLC.

Published by Tate Publishing & Enterprises, LLC
127 E. Trade Center Terrace | Mustang, Oklahoma 73064 USA
1.888.361.9473 | www.tatepublishing.com

Tate Publishing is committed to excellence in the publishing industry. The company reflects the philosophy established by the founders, based on Psalm 68:11,
"The Lord gave the word and great was the company of those who published it."

Book design copyright © 2014 by Tate Publishing, LLC. All rights reserved.
Cover design by Joseph Emnace
Interior design by Manolito Bastasa

Published in the United States of America

ISBN: 978-1-63367-490-5
1. Religion / Christian Church / Growth
2. Religion / Sermons / General
14.09.04

This book is dedicated to the very special women in my life—my wife, Nicole, and four girls Emma, Lily, Shiloh, and Hannah. You girls mean the world to me, and I am amazed that the Lord has given me the desire of my heart. All I have ever wanted to be was a loving husband and a good father. I pray that comes to pass. You have supported me in the work of God and are my greatest cheerleaders. I am so thankful for all of you and am truly blessed. I look forward to the day when we get to travel and minister together as a family.

It is also my desire that I would leave a legacy behind for my children. I've always wanted to leave footsteps behind for the four of you to follow. But I pray that as you grow in the things of God and in your own relationship with Him, the steps you take will eclipse mine. Indeed, my heart's desire is that you wouldn't fill my shoes but that you would outgrow them! I want every book I ever write and every journal I ever fill to be an example of how your father wrestled with and loved God. May my revelations be the floor you leap from and the encouragement to dig even deeper and discover all that God has for you.

I love you all.

Contents

Foreword

My husband Nic and I have had the incredible honor to know Brian and Nicole Connolly for several years. The Lord instantly connected our hearts. As a wife and proud mother of four children, I was naturally impacted by the tender way Brian and his wife nurture and care for their four beautiful daughters. Even the careful attention they put into naming them was done as a strategic way to prophesy destiny into each one. There is such an atmosphere of peace and acceptance in their home that only comes from hearts that have been radically overcome by the Father's love. My own father was a United Methodist pastor for all of my life, and something he always said really stuck with me. He said, "You'll know the way a pastor will shepherd his church by the way he shepherds his family." This is profoundly true in watching how Brian and his wife love the "one" in front of them and serve from the humble place at the feet of Jesus. His church at Praise Community continues to be a home away from home for my family when we are in the United States to minister.

When I heard Brian was writing another book, I was so excited! I knew it would be powerful! The revelations in this book seem to wrap around your heart and pull you into attention for where the kingdom of God is moving. What is the Lord saying to us in this time? What is He requiring of us as the mature sons and daughters? Are we as the church ready for the harvest of the lost ones to come home? All of these questions came flooding into my heart as I read *Awakened*. There is a call to us as the bride to wake up and make ourselves ready.

Nic and I are missionaries to Brazil and the founders and directors of our ministry, Shores of Grace. We open homes for woman and children who are rescued out of abuse and prostitution. We have the opportunity to fellowship with the poor and declare hope to the broken in the darkest of places. We have seen lives restored and we, as missionaries, are watching the nation God has given us be transformed. After these women and children have encountered the love of Christ in a real and tangible way, they become the conduits for transformation around them. Brian shares true stories from scripture of several women in the Bible that had one moment with The Lord and they were set free and became city changers and history makers that we still talk about today. These are the stories I hold so close to my heart on the streets in Brazil.

The combination of personal struggle and victory along with the beautiful illustrations from scripture will challenge you to get ready for everything the Lord has for you.

Awakened is a wake up call to the church. It's time, beautiful warrior bride! Arise, take off your grave clothes. You've been called, you've been chosen in Him! Now let's go boldly and not only proclaim the good news; let's live the good news to each one we encounter so that they will encounter Him!

—Rachael Billman
Cofounder and Codirector
Shores of Grace
Recife, Brazil

Prologue

Fall Afresh
by Jeremy Riddle[1]

[1] Awaken my soul, come awake
To hunger, to seek, to thirst
Awaken first love, come awake
And do as you did, at first

Spirit of the living God come fall afresh on me
Come wake me from my sleep
Blow through the caverns of my soul, pour in me to
overflow
To overflow

Spirit, come and fill this place
Let Your glory now invade
Spirit, come and fill this place
Let Your glory now invade

There's Something in a Title

I love the title of this book. I believe it captures what it is that is currently happening and is yet to happen within the body of Christ. It's where God is taking us and what many people are currently experiencing. We are waking up by the Spirit of God.

Our time of hibernation is coming to an end. God is calling us to arise from our slumber and rub the dust from our eyes.

This is not about a revival.

This is about an awakening.

Anything that is revived can once again return to the state it was revived from. You can revive a human heart, but that heart will inevitably cease to beat. People who are fully awake and fully alive, however, are incapable of falling asleep. *They're wide awake. They're alive.*

This is what God is after. This is what his voice is calling for and what creation groans for—the sons and daughters of God to come forth in maturity.

Truthfully, I believe that many people have sensed deep within themselves that something is coming. There is a growing dissatisfaction within many believers about where they are at and with what they have experienced with God. They know there's something more, and they've grown weary of learning. They want to live. They want to become. They want what they read within the scriptures to be their reality.

Within this book is one of my favorite stories in the Bible—the woman caught in adultery—and I believe it's an accurate depiction of how many people feel within their relationship with God. They feel stuck and frustrated, caught between what they've experienced and have come to understand and the reality that they are hungry and desperate for more. They have an itch that seemingly cannot be scratched by anything or anyone else but God Himself.

On June 13–15, 2013, I had the awesome privilege of being a part of a conference at Global Awakening's Apostolic Resource Center called "The Pursuit."[2] David Wagner of Fathers Heart Ministries, along with Will Hart, Bob Hazlett, and me, was one of the speakers at this two day, three night event. During one of David's sessions, he said these words that encapsulated everything that I had been feeling and am still feeling up to this point in my life. He said this:

This is a season of frustration and agitation... Do you know what I heard the Lord say? "It's not the enemy. And it's not you. It's Me." I believe there is a holy frustration that God is putting and releasing upon some of us because unless you felt that frustration, you would never change. Unless you would feel yourself getting frustrated you would just stay in the place of comfort.

I've never felt more frustrated. I've never had a greater desire within my heart to love people. I've never had a greater desire to know Him more. I'm hungry. I'm desperate. I want my life to be an echo of the same ambitions that Paul describes as his own in the following verses:

More than that, I count all things to be loss in view of the surpassing value of knowing Christ Jesus my Lord, for whom I have suffered the loss of all things, and count them but rubbish so that I may gain Christ, and may be found in Him, not having a righteousness of my own derived from *the* Law, but that which is through faith in Christ, the righteousness which *comes* from God on the basis of faith, *that I may know Him and the power of His resurrection and the fellowship of His sufferings, being conformed to His death*; in order that I may attain to the resurrection from the dead. Not that I have already obtained *it* or have already become perfect, but *I press on so that I may lay hold of that for which also I was laid hold of by Christ Jesus* (emphasis mine).

Philippians 3:8–12

I want to *become* like Jesus. I do not only want to know the power of His resurrection. I want to know the fellowship of His sufferings because He learned obedience through them. (See Hebrews 5:8.) I want to be conformed to the image of His death. I do not want to live for myself. I want to die to everything life ever taught me and be transformed by the renewing of my mind. (See Romans 12:2.) Life, paradoxically speaking for the Christian, is found in death. You come alive when love is at the center of all you do and when that wretched thing called "self" is dead and buried with no hope of being resurrected.

The year 2013 has opened my eyes to the fact that I need to believe the gospel in a greater way. I need to *see*. I need to *believe*. I'm tired of playing games. I'm tired of confessions. We say so much and live so little…I want to live! I want all that He is to overtake me. I'm no longer satisfied with knowledge. I must become just like *Him*. The things written in this book have not been written to walk you through steps. They've been written to confront you, challenge you, stretch you, and cause you to come alive in a greater way. They've been written so that you may gain insight into what God is doing in my life in hopes that you'll join me on this journey.

The reason, I believe, that many people feel stuck is because we as the body of Christ are in a time of noticeable transition. Although it would also be sufficient to say that we are always in a time of transition because we are constantly maturing and God is finishing the work within us that He started. (See Philippians 1:6.) During times of transition, anticipation rises. Hunger emerges. Groaning is stirred up from within. And I also believe as David Wagner has already pointed out that we are experiencing frustration in the midst of transition. Frustration produces desperation and desperation causes us to ask until our vocal chords become hoarse. Desperation causes us to beat on the door of heaven with bloodied knuckles. Desperation causes us to seek until we find what we are looking for, even if it means collapsing from exhaustion once we've found it.

It's not that people are purposing to feel frustrated. They simply know that something is coming. They are expecting. Second Corinthians 3:18 refers to this time of transition in this way: "But we all, with unveiled face, beholding as in a mirror the glory of the Lord, are being transformed into the same image from *glory to glory*, just as from the Lord, the Spirit (emphasis mine)."

I also believe that one of the reasons people feel stuck is because many of us have yet to truly experience what it is we say we believe with our mouths. Whether we realize it or not, so many of us have been educated way past our level of obedience. What I mean by that is we seem to know so much as Christians and yet live so little of what we claim we know. We do not need to learn any more than we already have. If knowledge was the answer, wouldn't this world look different by now? What we need is repentance. We need to change our minds. We need confronted with the reality that we deep down do not believe what we say we do. If we really believed, our lives would look completely different.

We've been taught all the right answers. We can quote Bible verses. We can reference the countless notes we have taken over the years from listening to various ministers. But my question to all of us is, When do we *become* what we claim we know? At what point in time are we willing to wrestle with such scriptures as the ones below?

> But prove yourselves doers of the word, and not merely hearers who delude themselves. For if anyone is a hearer of the word and not a doer, he is like a man who looks at his natural face in a mirror; for *once* he has looked at himself and gone away, he has immediately forgotten what kind of person he was.
>
> James 1:22–24

We cannot afford to keep hearing and keep learning and never *living*…never *becoming*. The last thing we need is more knowledge so that we can become puffed up or impressed with what we think we know (see 1 Cor. 8:1). I use the phrase "what we think we know" because the evidence of what we know isn't based upon our ability to fill our heads with information, pass exams, and talk a good game. The evidence of what we know is seen through the way we live, not through word only.

"Little children, let us not love with word or with tongue, but in deed and truth" (1 John 3:18).

"Even so faith, if it has no works, is dead, *being* by itself" (Jas. 2:17).

Jesus didn't die in order that we might become scholars and debate doctrine and sit in all the right circles and impress others and ourselves by our ability to "quote the word." He died for a reason. "Truly, truly, I say to you, unless a grain of wheat falls into the earth and dies, it remains alone; but if it dies, it bears much fruit" (John 12:24).

He died to reproduce Himself in us. He wasn't simply buried in the ground. He was a seed, *the Seed*, planted in the ground that died and rose again so that those who received Him could be born again by His seed and become the sons and daughters of God. (See 1 Peter 1:23 and John 1:12.) He died so that those who were dead themselves could come alive! He died so we could *become* just like Him! (See Romans 8:29.)

Christianity is about the transformation of life, not the accumulation of facts in order to persuade men or win arguments. It's about being born again by the power of the Spirit so that you might look like the Father who has adopted you. (See John 3:5, Romans 8:5, and Ephesians 1:5.) Paul greatly understood this, which is why he wrote what he wrote below to the church at Corinth.

> And when I came to you, brethren, I did not come with superiority of speech or of wisdom, proclaiming to you the testimony of God. For I determined to know nothing among you except Jesus Christ, and Him crucified. I was with you in weakness and in fear and in much trembling, and my message and my preaching were not in persuasive words of wisdom, but in demonstration of the Spirit and of power, so that your faith would not rest on the wisdom of men, but on the power of God.
>
> 1 Corinthians 2:1–5

Christianity is more than a confession. It's a life lived. It's not enough to say we believe something. The demons could do that and look where it got them!

"You believe that God is one. You do well; the demons also believe, and shudder" (James 2:19).

Please don't misunderstand what I'm saying. I'm not trying to bring anyone's salvation into question. But I am asking that we take a long, hard look at ourselves and do the very thing Paul is commanding the Corinthians to do.

"Test yourselves *to see* if you are in the faith; examine yourselves!" (2 Corinthians 13:5).

Indeed, I do believe that the reason why so many Christians "feel stuck," frustrated, hungry, and desperate is we've acquired knowledge without application and obedience. A great example of what I am referring to can be taken from the lyrics of the song "I Still Haven't Found What I'm Looking For" by Irish rock band U2. In this song, Bono, the band's lead singer, writes and sings these words:

I have spoke with the
tongue of angels
I have held the hand of a devil
It was warm in the night
I was cold as a stone.

But I still haven't found
What I'm looking for.
But I still haven't found
What I'm looking for.

I believe in the Kingdom Come
Then all the colours
will bleed into one

Bleed into one.
But yes, I'm still running.

You broke the bonds
And you loosed the chains
Carried the cross of my shame
Oh my shame, you
know I believe it.

But I still haven't found
What I'm looking for.

How is it possible for someone to speak in the tongue of an angel (1 Cor. 13:1), believe in the kingdom come, and that Jesus carried the cross, bearing their shame and breaking the bonds and loose the chains of sin and conclude that they still haven't found what they're looking for? I believe the answer lies within what he *claims* he believes.

Come on, guys. Think with me for a moment. If Bono truly believed in the lyrics he's written, he wouldn't be searching. How could he? He would have understood that he's been found and that the search ends with the One who finds you. But I believe that Bono's words are an accurate depiction of how many Christians are living today. So many Christians are still searching. They want to be significant. They're longing to be loved. They want to know why they exist and what their purpose is.

Could you imagine if we just believed in the songs we sing? Could you imagine if we believed in the creeds we can quote? Could you imagine if we really, really, really believed in the same things Bono is claiming he believes in? I can promise you, our lives would look radically different. We'd start to live and look just like the One who said, "Follow Me."

Please keep in mind that I am not promoting a work-based Christianity. The last thing we need to do is "get busy" out of a sense of condemnation over the incongruence in our lives between what we say and actually do. You don't read about the Christian life and then bite your lip and try to do it. It's something you walk out when we understand who we already are through the finished work of the cross and through the eyes of God. It's something you become by His grace through faith. And I believe that it's time for us to seek and to pray until the things we claim we believe burn like fire within us. If our God is a consuming fire (see Hebrews 12:29), then His children ought to look like one as well. It's through communion with God and fellowship with the Holy Spirit that the eyes of our understanding are opened. We need revelation, not information. It's time we humble ourselves and get real and draw near to Him so that He will draw near to us. (See James 4:8.)

It's time we seek so we can find.

Why This Book?

In fact, my goal in writing this book is to increase your understanding and my hope is that this book would serve as a catalyst to transition you from glory *to* glory. I pray that these words would serve as jumper cables that the Holy Spirit connects to your heart to cause you to come alive in a greater way. It's time that we'd be fully awake. It's time we start acting upon what we say with our mouths. It's time to seek Him in the same manner and intensity that He's sought us.

I want to bring you face-to-face, once again, with the reality of what Jesus did on our behalf and what that means for you and I want to challenge you to believe, because the time is *now*. It's time to see. It's time to believe. We must unite what we have heard with faith. We must be fully awake and fully alive. This is why Hebrews 2:1 says, "For this reason we must pay much closer attention to what we have heard, so that we do not drift away *from it.*"

Indeed, this book is about many things, and it's been written to cause us to wake up in a greater way. It's actually the conglomeration of everything God had spoken to me throughout the course of 2013.

It's about faith and real life examples and testimonies.

It's about prayer and intimacy.

It's about understanding your identity and value.

It's about His coming and mission.

It's about beauty and how personal the gospel truly is.

It's about coming awake.

It's about dying to live.

Most of all, it's about helping every reader to believe and to see the reality of what Jesus has done on our behalf through the glory of the gospel. And I can think of no greater example of beauty than God humbling Himself to become like the ones He created to say with vocal chords He formed and through a mouth He designed, "I love you. I forgive you. You are mine."

I sometimes think about the fact that the One who knows the stars by name and number (Isa. 40:26) and can hold the water of the earth in the palm of His hand and who measures the universe by the breadth of His hand (Isa. 40:12) came to world He created to find me and to save me.

He really came; that alone should cause us to stop doing what we are doing and think upon that reality.

Among other things, I use the personal stories of three beautiful and amazing women from the Bible to convey this truth. Their stories have been my personal favorite stories for quite some time. They embody the heartbeat of the gospel. They are the fabric woven in the garment of His grace. They are the strokes of God's paintbrush that contribute to the unveiling of His ultimate masterpiece: the redemption of man.

The truth is that I've been waiting quite some time for the same feeling I had within me when I had written my first book, *First Dance: Venturing Deeper into a Relationship with God* before attempting to write this one you hold in your hands. I have sat down and tried to write many times since the completion of *First Dance* but to no avail. Every attempt felt forced. It felt like my own effort and not the empowerment of His grace. When the idea for my first book had come to me, I felt like I was going to explode if I didn't write it. It had to get out. It had to be released. I finally feel that way once again. And that feeling has now produced the words you are reading.

My Hope and Prayer for You

My hope and desire is that the words upon the pages you hold will be like seeds that God will use to plant within your heart.

I pray that the content of this book will be reproduced within your own life and be multiplied through you in the lives of others. I pray that His grace will find you in a greater way as you interact with and meditate upon every scripture, every testimony, and every story you encounter. I pray that understanding will abound and knowledge will increase that leads to growth within you.

I'm always amazed at how God allows us to glean from others through one book, sermon, or teaching in such a short amount of time what took years for the author, preacher, or teacher to understand. That's His grace. It's no different than the landowner hiring laborers to work in his vineyard at different times of the day and everyone getting paid the same amount (Matt. 20:1–16). Some worked all day. Some worked for only one hour. The wages were the same.

It's my joy and honor to sow into your life through what has been given to me in understanding through seeking, asking, and knocking and from walking through the fire of trials. Be blessed as you read. Be transformed as your mind is renewed through truth. And may the following prayer of Paul become a reality in your life.

> For this reason I too, having heard of the faith in the Lord Jesus which *exists* among you and your love for all the saints, do not cease giving thanks for you, while making mention *of you* in my prayers; that the God of our Lord Jesus Christ, the Father of glory, may give to you a spirit of wisdom and of revelation in the knowledge of Him. *I pray that* the eyes of your heart may be enlightened, so that you will know what is the hope of His calling, what are the riches of the glory of His inheritance in the saints, and what is the surpassing greatness of His power toward us who believe.
>
> Ephesians 1:15–19

Introduction

For this reason I bow my knees before the Father, from whom every family in heaven and on earth derives its name, that He would grant you, according to the riches of His glory, to be strengthened with power through His Spirit in the inner man, so that Christ may dwell in your hearts through faith; *and* that you, being rooted and grounded in love, may be able to comprehend with all the saints what is the breadth and length and height and depth, [19] and to know the love of Christ which surpasses knowledge, that you may be filled up to all the fullness of God.

Ephesians 3:14–19

Every priest stands daily ministering and offering time after time the same sacrifices, which can never take away sins; but He, having offered one sacrifice for sins for all time, *sat down at the right hand of God*, waiting from that time onward *until His enemies be made a footstool for his feet.* For by one offering He has perfected for all time those who are sanctified.

Hebrews 10:1–14

"It is finished!"

John 19:30

We Are Not Ignorant of His Schemes

My whole life, all I've ever wanted was found at the feet of Jesus. I just didn't know it. I had given myself to so many things. I prostituted my created value. I had cast my pearls before swine (Matt. 7:6). I got into bed with food, lying, stealing, drugs, pornography, and the approval of people. The truth is that I never would have given myself to those things if I understood the value of my life or how my Father saw me.

I tried it all, believing it all to be the answer to my dilemma—*me.* Truly, for the majority of my life, I did not know the love of Christ that Paul is referring to in the verses from his letter to the Ephesians above or did I truly understand the beauty of forgiveness. I did not know that what I was created for and searching for was the very thing that was causing him to hit his knees to pray on behalf of all people. Nowhere else in Scripture do we read about Paul posturing himself in such a way before the Father. Nowhere else in his letters do we see such intensity behind the point he is trying to make. Paul is praying that we'd come to know the very thing people have been looking for the moment we were separated from it in a garden called Eden, the love of Christ. It's the knowing of this love that causes us to be filled up to all the fullness of God! And the reality and magnitude of this love was communicated through the death of God's own Son (see John 15:13) for the forgiveness of sin.

As much as Paul is praying that people would come to know it, there's someone else lurking behind the scenes to ensure that we don't. Peter talks about this person in this way: "Your adversary, the devil, prowls around like a roaring lion, seeking someone to devour" (1 Pet. 5:8).

Jesus says this about the same guy. "The thief comes only to steal and kill and destroy" (John 10:10).

And Paul gives us great insight into this same person's strategy by revealing these words:

> And even if our gospel is veiled, it is veiled to those who are perishing, in whose case the god of this world has blinded the minds of the unbelieving so that they might not see the light of the gospel of the glory of Christ, who is the image of God.
>
> 2 Corinthians 4:3–4

The last thing Satan wants is for the "light" to come on in your life. He doesn't want you to *see* the gospel. He doesn't want you having what He can't have—redemption, reconciliation, forgiveness, love, intimacy, and acceptance. The enemy knows that if we ever learn to see ourselves and God clearly through the gospel, it's game over for him. To know who you are and whose you are through the good news of Jesus Christ is a sign of destruction to your opponents, the powers of darkness (Phil. 1:28). Why? Because you are no longer moved by life and how it seems and how it's going. It no longer has any power of you. You know who you are and better yet, you know who He (God) is.

To know the love of God is everything because you come alive through it. You are led to repentance because of it. But in an effort to blind you to it, Satan doesn't simply put a blindfold over your eyes. There's no wool he's trying to pull over you. Rather, he seeks to blind you by getting you to *see* everything else but the light of the gospel of the glory of Christ. He seeks to wound the very thing that Jesus came to bind and where belief resides—the heart. (See Isaiah 61:1 and Psalm 14:1.) He wants you to see with your eyes and think with your mind. God wants you to hear with your ears and believe with your heart.

It Is Finished

Satan always seeks to bring into question everything that God has said in an effort to get you to see a different reality and to persuade you to take matters into your own hands. His whole goal is to get you to agree with what he is *saying* in an effort to keep you from what has been *said.* In the beginning, God made man in His image. The crafting of the image of God in man was finished in the garden and yet the enemy had brought this finished work into question by raising doubt within Eve. Let's take a look at this story together

> Now the serpent was more crafty than any beast of the field which the LORD God had made. And he said to the woman, "Indeed, has God said, 'You shall not eat from any tree of the garden '?" The woman said to the serpent, "From the fruit of the trees of the garden we may eat; but from the fruit of the tree which is in the middle of the garden, God has said, 'You shall not eat from it or touch it, or you will die.'" The serpent said to the woman, "You surely will not die! "For God knows that in the day you eat from it your eyes will be opened, and you will be like God, knowing good and evil." When the woman saw that the tree was good for food, and that it was a delight to the eyes, and that the tree was desirable to make *one* wise, she took from its fruit and ate; and she gave also to her husband.
>
> Genesis 3:1–6

Indeed, when the serpent said, "You will be like God," he was suggesting that Eve wasn't already made in God's likeness and image. So what did he do? He gave *her* something to do. She saw that the food that was forbidden and that would lead to death if she ate it as the source to becoming the very thing she already was—like God.

Satan will always give you something to do. Jesus will always give you something to believe. Jesus Himself said that the work of God is for us to believe in Him (John 6:29). The enemy wants the exact opposite. He wants you living by the strength of your own effort. Why? When you succeed, you become self-righteous. When you fail, you feel unworthy and condemned. It's older brother and younger brother stuff. (See Luke 15.) Both brothers saw themselves through what they did, not through who their father was and how he felt about them.

The enemy doesn't want you living by faith. He doesn't want you to see what God has done. He wants you to see how you've been treated by others. He doesn't want you to see what Christ has accomplished on your behalf. He wants you to see that there's still more for you to do.

When Jesus was hanging on the cross and inhaling and exhaling His final breaths of air, He uttered these three words before yielding up His spirit, "It is finished" (John 19:30). What's finished? What is "*it*"? "It" is everything that needed to happen for the forgiveness and atonement of my sin so that I could become brand new and live as if sin never touched me and as if I had never been sinned against. "It" is everything that needed to happen to make a way home for me and so I could see myself for who I really am. "It" is everything the Son of God was willing to do in order to save the image and our standing with Him that we lost through sin.

If we release faith in anything less than "it is finished," we will always try to finish "it." We will try to make lovely what's been made lovely. We will seek to make acceptable what's been accepted. And we will petition Him to forgive what's already been forgiven.

Satan always seeks to attack and bring into question the finished work of Christ. If we would dare to believe that He has offered one sacrifice for *sins* (plural) for all time (Hebrews 10:12), the enemy would have no rocks to throw at us. The certificate of debt that he seeks to hold against us would lose its voice when we see that it has been nailed to the cross (Col. 2:14). We have been forgiven!

Indeed, if the enemy can get you to see everything but Christ (the source of our salvation, the very image of God, the very light of the gospel), he can begin to talk to you about what you do *see*. There has been a strategy set against us the moment we came forth from our mother's womb. Satan has sought to harden our hearts through life so that by the time we hear the good news, we either don't understand it, want nothing to do with it, or think it's too good to be true. But it's not too good to be true. It's *the* truth (John 14:6)!

The enemy wants you to believe that the truth about you and about God is not what Christ came to reveal, but what life taught you. Truly, whatever I saw with my eyes became an opportune time for Satan to come alongside of me and whisper lies to me. Because his lies always made sense or seemed right in light of how I was being treated or what I was going through, I believed them. There is a way that seems right to a man, but its end is the way of death (Prov. 14:12). As a result, I saw everything through the lies I allowed to be sown in the soil of my heart. I saw myself through them. I saw God through them. And I saw everyone else through them.

Life taught me many things. It was a terrible, cruel, and unjust teacher. It taught me that I wasn't good enough and that I was worthy of rejection. It instructed me in the ways of performance. It coached me to crave the very thing that seemed to elude me— man's approval. As a result, I lived my life like a mouse running on a wheel or a dog chasing its own tail. I was trapped in the rat race of life. The only problem is that when you win, you're still a rat!

I was caught in a vicious cycle. I believed that I needed people to like me to feel good about myself. Rejection hurt, so I would strive to be accepted. I did whatever I had to do. I'd lie. I'd show off. I'd put others down. I did things I didn't want to do as long as it meant I'd receive instant gratification through acceptance. I was clay in the hands of those whom I wanted to approve of me. If they'd say jump, I'd say, "How high?" I was whoever *you* wanted me to be.

Deep down, I didn't want to live this way. It was the only way I knew. It was the only way I was familiar with. It was exhausting. Keeping up appearances was more tiring than all of my lacrosse practices put together at Millersville University. If someone rejected me, their disapproval sent a signal to my brain telling me that I needed to try harder. Their rejection also reinforced the very lie(s) I had believed about myself, that no one really liked me and that I would be alone. Indeed, the very thing that rejected me became the object of my desire.

The rejection I experienced in life had many lies attached to it. One of the greatest lies I had believed was this: If you reject me or don't like me, that means I'm not good enough. If I'm not good enough, I can't even like myself. If I can't like myself, I certainly can't forgive myself.

I hated that it seemed like I wasn't accepted. I hated working so hard to be loved and noticed. At the core of my being, I think I even hated myself. How could I love the very thing that everyone seemed to turn up their nose to?

Do You Love What You See?

The lies I had believed about myself came to a climax one afternoon in my basement in the year of 2008. It was the crescendo of the symphony of my life that had been playing bad notes all of my days up to this point. I had mentioned this moment before in my first book, *First Dance: Venturing Deeper into a Relationship with God.* I was reading a book by Joyce Meyer[1] entitled *Approval Addiction.* Somewhere within the pages of the book, Joyce asks you to participate in an odd request. As you're reading, she instructs you to stop and to wrap your arms around yourself and tell yourself these words: "I love you."

I was nowhere near prepared for what happened next after I read those three simple words. What seemed so easy to do and seemed to require no effort was impossible for me. I couldn't do it. I couldn't wrap my arms around myself and say, "I love you." I didn't love myself.

And it scared me.

It was *the* defining moment in my life because it forced me to come to grips with the very thing I had been running from and living in denial with. I didn't like myself. God never taught me that. Life did. I had shaken hands with how I was treated and what had been said about me for so long that I saw myself through every demeaning word and every cruel act. If you couldn't like me, how could I like me? The sad thing is that I wanted everyone to like and to love the very thing I didn't—*me*.

This is what I mean when I say that there has been a strategy from the enemy set against you and me from the beginning. He had sought to get me so filled with hurt, anger, unforgiveness, self-loathing, and self-pity so that by the time I heard the good news that God loves me and forgives me, I wouldn't be able to receive it.

Ironic, isn't it?

The very thing we want we sometimes push away because we don't believe we are worthy of it.

The Power of Conviction

Here is a verse that I'm sure I'll reference quite a bit throughout this book: "Now faith is the assurance of *things* hoped for, the conviction of things not seen" (Heb. 11:1).

To have a conviction implies that you are utterly convinced of something. It's good to be absolutely convinced that God loves you. We know that God loves us because He sent His Son (John 3:16). We know what love is because 1 John 4:10 says, "In this is love, not that we loved God, but that He loved us and sent His Son to be the propitiation for our sins." To have a conviction that God loves you in the context of the verse above implies that even when you can't see the love of God with your natural eyes or feel it, you are assured and convinced that He does. In other words, even when the world is falling apart around you and no one is singing your praise, you have a hope that's an anchor for your soul. It's a revelation you carry in your heart. It's more than something you feel. It's something you have a history with. It's been written on the fleshly tablet of your heart. "God loves me."

The reality is that faith is always being released somewhere. It's like my friend Tyler McCarty once said to me. "There's no such thing as unbelief," he explained. "Unbelief is simply belief in the wrong things." For the great majority of my life, I placed my faith in everything else but what God had spoken to me through His Son. My faith was placed in what life had spoken to me.

"So faith *comes* from hearing, and hearing by the word of Christ" (Rom. 10:17).

The truth is that everything in life has a voice, and whichever voice you release faith in will become the eyes you see through. If faith comes from hearing, and hearing by the word of Christ, faith is conceived through fellowship. It's birthed relationally with God. This is why intimacy with God is important. We can no longer afford to be intimate with how we were treated or what we've been through. We must become intimate with the love of God because faith works *through* it (Gal. 5:6).

A great example of what it looks like to release faith in the wrong things is found in the way anorexics see themselves. Sadly, they can look in the mirror and even though the mirror is reflecting a severely malnourished frame, they will still see an overweight person. They are convinced they are heavy. Why? Because it's a conviction they carry. They are convinced that they need to lose weight. They are incapable of seeing the damage of what they have done to their own bodies because they see themselves for what they believe about themselves.

Similarly, I saw myself through the conviction of everything life had taught me apart from the truth revealed through Jesus Christ. Even when I was treated contrary to what I believed about myself by others, I still saw myself for what I believed about me.

Unworthy.

Unlovable.

Unwanted.

I was convinced that I was those things. I had released faith in the wrong voices. I bought the lie, and it shaped me and molded me until the day when the light came on within me.

The Light Is Already Shining

"The people who were sitting in darkness saw a great light, and those who were sitting in the land and shadow of death, upon them a light dawned" (Matt. 4:16).

John wrote this concerning Jesus: "In Him was life, and the life was the Light of men" (John 1:4). He is the Light. The cool thing about the light is that it removes darkness. You can *see* because of the Light. Truth is revealed through it and truth crushes every lie. Why? Fellowship with the light causes illumination. I can see who I am and who He is clearly through the Light and it causes me to come alive. Life is in Him. Everything we have been looking for is in Him. We can wake up because the Light is already shining.

Throughout the latter part of 2013, I, and many others, have been seeing the number 11 everywhere. I am not joking. I see it on clocks. The time will often be 11:11 a.m. or p.m. or 1:11 p.m. (I'm usually not awake at 1:11 a.m.) I'll read it on the clock on my night stand. I'll read it on the clock on my phone. I'll read it on the clock inside my car. In fact, just the other day as I was driving home from the office, my odometer read 111,100 miles. When I got in my car to drive back to the office the very next day, my odometer read 111,111 miles. It's exactly 11 miles from the church to my house. *Ah!* You can't make this stuff up! It haunts me! iTunes even asked me if I wanted to update to their newer version 11.1.1 the other day!

Since the time I began to notice that the number 11 was showing up everywhere, the Lord had been talking to me about faith and its importance. (See Hebrews 11.) More than that, He directed me to John 11:11. "This He [Jesus] said, and after that He said to them, *Our friend Lazarus has fallen asleep; but I go, so that I may awaken him out of sleep*" (emphasis mine).

In order to understand in a greater way what Jesus is referring to here in the verse above, let's look at it in its context:

Now a certain man was sick, Lazarus of Bethany, the village of Mary and her sister Martha. It was the Mary who anointed the Lord with ointment, and wiped His feet with her hair, whose brother Lazarus was sick. So the sisters sent *word* to Him, saying, "Lord, behold, he whom You love is sick." But when Jesus heard *this*, He said, "This sickness is not to end in death, but for the glory of God, so that the Son of God may be glorified by it." Now Jesus loved Martha and her sister and Lazarus. So when He heard that he was sick, He then stayed two days *longer* in the place where He was. Then after this He said to the disciples, "Let us go to Judea again." The disciples said to Him, "Rabbi, the Jews were just now seeking to stone You, and are You going there again?" Jesus answered, "Are there not twelve hours in the day? If anyone walks in the day, he does not stumble, because he sees the light of this world. "But if anyone walks in the night, he stumbles, because the light is not in him." This He said, and after that He said to them, "Our friend Lazarus has fallen asleep; but I go, so that I may awaken him out of sleep."

John 11:1–11

Prophetically speaking, I believe that Lazarus represents the church in this particular season and time. The body of Christ is *sick* at large. We fight and argue with one another more than we love one another. We gossip and bicker, divorce one another, and often times look no different than the world. We live out of our past and hurt rather than faith. We are more concerned about defending our doctrines and theological stances than finding common ground and understanding that we are here for the same reason—to manifest Jesus Christ on the earth. We hold conferences to "call out" those within the body of Christ that don't think like us or look like us while arrogantly believing that our way of thinking is superior. We value being "right" more than we do being righteous, and people are turned off.

The lost are not beating down our doors to get in. Why would they want to come into a place that looks just like the world they are already apart of? In his book *What's So Amazing About Grace?*, author Philip Yancey[2] shares the following story he had heard from a friend who works with the down-and-out in Chicago:

> A prostitute came to me in wretched straits, homeless, sick, unable to buy food for her two-year-old daughter. Through sobs and tears, she told me she had been renting out her daughter – two years old! – to men interested in kinky sex. She made more renting out her daughter for an hour than she could earn on her own in a night. She had to do it, she said, to support her own drug habit. I could hardly bear hearing her sordid story. For one thing, it made me legally liable – I'm required to report cases of child abuse. I had no idea what to say to this woman.
>
> At last I asked if she had ever thought of going to a church for help. I will never forget the look of pure, naïve shock that crossed her face. "Church!" she cried. "Why would I ever go there? I was already feeling terrible about myself. They'd just make me feel worse."

That's some indictment, huh? But it's true. I'll never forget the first time I read about this woman's story. It's one of those things that just kind of sticks with you. You can't forget about it no matter how hard you try. I remember feeling so angry toward this woman. I'm the father of four girls and I could not imagine doing to them what this woman did with her two-year-old daughter. As I read her story, all I could think about was my girls being forced to do the unthinkable against their will. But the truth is this mother knows no other way. She's lost, so lost. And she doesn't know who or where to turn to, and it's a pretty sad day for us as the body of Christ when women like this mother used to run to Jesus but are unwilling to run to Him today. Let's face it, words such as *full of grace, loving, compassionate,* and *merciful* are rarely heard when you ask the average person what they think about when they think about Christians. We are known more for our judgment and strong moral convictions than we are for our unconditional love and heart to serve. This needs to change. We must repent.

In fact, more and more church doors are closing every year in America. If we are truly honest, many people would look upon the church and see it the way the disciples saw Lazarus: *dead*! And yet, God never sees things the way man sees them, does He? In fact, Jesus said that Lazarus's sickness would not end in death but for the glory of God. Jesus loves the church. It's His bride, and He will be glorified through it. This sickness within the body of Christ will not end in death but for the glory of God!

God never weighs a book by its cover. He sees a greater reality. He sees below the surface. What we see as dead, He sees as asleep and ready to awaken. This is why He asks the prophet Ezekiel if the bones Ezekiel is walking among in the valley can live (Ezek. 37:1–3). Ezekiel, being the smart man that he is, responds to the Lord and says, "O Lord God, You know." He's right. The Lord always knows the answer to every question He's asking. He's asking to find out if you know the answer. He's inviting you into what He sees and how He thinks. It's what Romans 12:2 refers to as being transformed by the *renewing* of your mind.

Take note that in verse nine of John 11, Jesus makes mention that there are twelve hours in the day. What if the reason I and so many have been seeing the number eleven is because we are in the eleventh hour? What if a great awakening is upon us? What if the church, like Lazarus, is getting ready to rise up? I do believe the reason that God directed me to John 11:11 was so He could show me that it's time for the church to awaken. I believe we are about to step into our finest hour, the twelfth hour. I believe the church is about to unite what it has heard with faith and that we are going to become a different breed of people. In fact, the reason why Jesus was so deeply moved in spirit in John 11 had nothing to do with the death of Lazarus. Why would Jesus weep (see John

11:35) over someone He was about to raise from the dead? He wept over the unbelief of the people around Him. The resurrection and the life (see John 11:25) was standing before them and all the people could see was death. All they could think about was the fact that Lazarus was decomposing and more than likely was starting to smell a little ripe behind the stone that encased him.

After Martha cautions Him about the stench that could pierce their nostrils because her brother had been dead for four days, "Jesus said to her, 'Did I not say to you that *if you believe*, you will see the glory of God?'" (John 11:40).

Now more than ever, Jesus is asking us to believe. He doesn't want us to be focused on what's happening around us. He wants our eyes on Him. He doesn't want us to see dry bones. He wants us to see an army. (See Ezekiel 37:1–10.) And He wants us to declare what it is we see through His eyes. He wants us to command what we see to come alive!

It's also significant to point out that in verse 6 of John 11, Jesus purposefully stayed two more days where He was after the news of Lazarus's death reached Him. Second Peter 3:8 tells us that with the Lord one day is like a thousand years and a thousand years like one day. Two days. Two thousand years. 2013. Please understand that I am in no way shape or form trying to imply or say that I know when it is that the Lord is coming back. What I'm saying is that I believe now is the time for Lazarus to arise. Now is the time for the church to see and to believe.

I believe Jesus is calling each and every one of us by name in the same way He called to Lazarus with a *loud voice*, "Lazarus, come forth." (See John 11:43.) We want to be a people who have ears to hear and eyes to see. The Lord is calling the things that are dead within you to life! Groanings are awakening and rising up within people. These groanings are the inward response to the calling of His voice. Hunger and thirst are rising. I believe that there is now more than ever a desire to know and be used by God. There is a holy frustration and discontentment within many people who are ready for more. And as we hear His voice,

He is causing us to take off everything that we are *not* in Him. He's awakening us to see who He is and who we really are and is clothing us with that reality. (See Colossians 3:10.)

"The man who had died came forth, bound hand and foot with wrappings, and his face was wrapped around with a cloth. Jesus said to them, 'Unbind him, and let him go'" (John 11:44).

It's time to take off rejection. It's time to take off disappointment and frustration. It's time to take off unforgiveness and bitterness. It's time to take off self-pity and self-righteousness. It's time to take off the past that is no longer yours that has been swallowed up by His mercy. It's time to take off the clothes of death and put on the garment of life. It's time to put on love.

My friend Nic Billman says it this way at the end of the extended version of his song, "The Invitation" from the album *In the Sound of Your Heartbeat*[3]:

> See, this is the thing… It's like you're alive. You've been born again. You've been set free. But some of us, despite all of that, are walking around wearing the clothes of a dead man. We are wearing the garments of a tomb that has yet to be opened instead of wearing the robes of righteousness that have been given to those who have walked through the empty tomb. And the world hears our message and we say, "We're alive! We've been set free." And they say, "Then why do your garments smell like death? Why are you still wearing the clothes of a dead man?"
>
> You see, garments have a funny way of becoming identity. You say, "See? I wear the garments of a beggar. I'm a beggar. This is who I am."
>
> …or the garments of a tomb. "I must be dead."
>
> "I wear this old, filthy dress. It must be all that I'm worth."
>
> And the Lord is saying to you tonight, "I've laid out garments of white sewn with grace and washed in blood. You don't have to wear those old rags anymore. You don't

have to wear that false identity anymore, because I've made you righteous. I've given you life. I've placed my very Spirit inside of you. I've given you life. Take off the clothes of a dead man. Put on the robes of righteousness. Son and daughter, I've called you by name. I'm calling you still saying, 'Come forth and take off the grave clothes.'"

The truth is that the world will not want what we claim we have if our garments smell like death. When was the last time someone asked you to give an account for the hope that is inside of you? (See 1 Peter 3:15.) In the same way that no one puts new wine into old wineskins because the skins will burst, you cannot patch up an old garment with a piece of cloth from a new garment because you will tear the new and the piece from the new will not match the old. (See Luke 5:36–37.) It's about a new garment, not patching up an old one. We aren't incorporating our new life through Christ with our former ways of living and believing. We aren't seeking to keep the old person alive. We die to live and we take off everything that we are not through Christ.

When Lazarus was raised from the dead, he came forward wrapped in the same garments that clothed him for burial. He was alive, but his wrappings declared a different reality. So many Christians today are alive by the Spirit of God but are still bound by hurt, pain, offense, and disappointment. We claim we know our identity with our mouth, but our life reveals something different. These are articles of clothing that no longer fit us as His sons and daughters. Jesus told those who were standing around to unbind Lazarus and to let him go. Jesus didn't do it. He told the witnesses, the onlookers, the crowd to do it and we need to do it for one another.

Earlier this year, I had made a decision I was avoiding for quite some time. I finally decided to deal with the contents in my closet! I'm not referring to the skeletons of a person's past that people often try to hide from others. I'm talking about the space that concealed a different kind of secret. Behind the fold-ing doors of the closet in my bedroom were shirts and pants that had hung on hangers, unworn for years. I actually had shirts and jeans that were leftover from 2004! I'm not sure if any of you can relate to this or not, but I was much thinner than I currently am. I had held on to this belief for the past nine years that I would lose weight and get back into wedding form! I looked so good in my wedding pictures! My hair was thicker and darker and I was fifty pounds lighter than I am now. A wife, a dog, four kids, and seven years later in full time ministry, I've arrived at the current state I'm in! For some reason, every time the kids eat, I think I need to eat right along with them. This is problematic for anyone who has identical twin girls who are infants and are eating every three to four hours. It's also problematic for the person who no longer has the time he once did to exercise! Please understand that I am in no way shape or form blaming my weight gain on the wonderful blessings God has given me. I understand that this is a time in my life where my time has to be devoted to other things, and I'm okay with that.

Despite my belief that I would once again look like my 2004 self, I finally got real with *me* and decided to get rid of the clothing that no longer fit me. I realized that there are plenty of people who could wear what I've been holding onto for nine years! I still believe that I will lose the weight, but in the meantime, I will continue to get rid of the garments I can no longer wear. I do not want to wear the garments of rejection and offense. I want the integrity of Jesus's life formed within my own life.

As much as I find the miracles of Jesus fascinating, I find His ability to remain unchanged in the face of the greatest rejection and injustice any one person has had to endure greater still. John 1:11 (there's that 11 again!) says that He came to His own, and those who were His own did not receive Him. Could you imagine that? The very people He created wanted nothing to do with Him and ultimately nailed Him to a cross and it never changed His heart toward them. Most of us fall apart if we find out that we are the topic of conversation within a circle we didn't attend or if someone didn't say "thank you" in recognition of a sacrifice we made. But that's what makes Jesus wonderful, isn't it? His love for you is never contingent upon your response toward Him. He's not waiting to be paid back or recognized for what He did. He's not falling apart, biting His nails because someone didn't pray today or read their Bible. He isn't angry, furrowing His brow because someone cursed His name and rejected Him.

He loves you. He doesn't have issues with you. Love gives. It doesn't wait to receive. He can't stop loving you. It's who He *is* and what you do will always flow out of who you *are*.

Let's be real. He was able to perceive the thoughts and intentions of every person's heart He encountered. He knew the Pharisees were trying to trap Him. He knew Judas would betray Him. He knew Thomas would doubt Him. He knew Peter would deny Him. And yet there He was in the thick of it with them, doing life, loving them, choosing them, and taking a nail for them. I want that kind of heart to *be* my reality. I want to respond to life that way. I don't want to *talk* a good game. I want to *live* a good game. I don't want to love people because of what they can do for me. I don't want to harden my heart because someone offended me. In fact, I tell people all the time that if I *feel* offended, I'm less interested in the offense the person committed toward me. I'm more interested in why it is that I feel offended. To me, the offense of the person isn't the issue; my response is, and I want to respond like heaven. I want the love of God.

No Greater Love

The truth is that we cannot *do* what Jesus *did* until we *do* what Jesus *did*. Confused? Let me explain. During the last Passover that Jesus would celebrate with His disciples (what many commonly refer to as the Last Supper), He did something out of character. When the meal was over, He got up, *laid aside His garments*, and girded Himself with a towel. He then poured water into a basin and began to wash the disciples' feet and to wipe them with the towel that now clothed Him. (See John 13:4–5.) Indeed, through this one act, Jesus summed up and revealed why it is that He came and the example He was leaving behind. (See John 13:15.) He didn't come to be served but to serve. (See Matthew 20:28.)

Jesus did nothing from selfishness or empty conceit. He did what He did with humility of mind, regarding everyone else as more important than Himself. He didn't look out for His own personal interests but also for the interests of others. He never used the fact that He existed in the form of God for personal gain. He never allowed His equality with God to result in special treatment. He emptied Himself and took on the form of a bond servant and was made in the likeness of men. Ironically, Paul urges us to do the same thing.

> Do nothing from selfishness or empty conceit, but with humility of mind regard one another as more important than yourselves; do not *merely* look out for your own personal interests, but also for the interests of others. Have this attitude in yourselves which was also in Christ Jesus, who, although He existed in the form of God, did not regard equality with God a thing to be grasped, but emptied Himself, taking the form of a bond-servant, *and* being made in the likeness of men.
>
> Philippians 2:3–7

But you can't *do* what Jesus *did* unless you *do* what Jesus *did*. Jesus was able to do what He did because love dominated Him. John 15:13 explains that the greatest demonstration of love is when someone lays their life down for someone else. But it's more than just dying on a cross. It's also evidenced through and contained in what Jesus did when He washed the disciples' feet. In doing so, He was saying, "This is why I came. I'm not in this thing for Me. I love you. This is what love looks like. It has no strings attached. It's not selfish. It overlooks a multitude of sin and it serves and honors the person standing before it. Follow my example."

Jesus removed His garments before washing His disciples' feet. We need to do the same thing. It's time to take off anger, wrath, malice, slander, and abusive speech. (See Colossians 3:8.) It's time to take off how people have treated you and put on how Christ has treated you. It's time to take off the garments of death and put on the garments of life. If we are still wearing these things it's because we are at the center of our own existence. You can only be offended if it's still about you. You can only be hurt if you're still alive. You can only feel rejected if you don't understand your acceptance through Christ. As long as these garments drape our frame, we can't love others. It's impossible. You will *need* people, not love them.

A Shift in Perspective

> The eye is the lamp of the body; so then if your eye is clear, your whole body will be full of light. But if your eye is bad, your whole body will be full of darkness. If then the light that is in you is darkness, how great is the darkness!
>
> Matthew 6:22–23

The last thing we need is to have a bad eye that causes us to be filled with darkness. If anything, these verses reveal that we were created for the light. We were created to see with a clear eye, the eye of truth. For most of my life, I saw myself with a bad eye. I was filled with lies. But God changed all of that. Something happens to a person when they discover that God loves the very thing they hate and wants the very thing they didn't want. Since the day God found me, I have often sat and meditated on these things. He wanted the very thing I was killing through drugs. He forgave the very person I had the hardest time forgiving— *me*. And He loved me not on the basis of my deeds, but according to who He is, according to His great mercy. Indeed, faith in these realities causes our eye to be clear and our bodies to be full of light.

Bono might sing U2's famous hit "I Still Haven't Found What I'm Looking For" but I have. I've found everything I was ever looking for and much more. I found the treasure hidden in the field. I've found the pearl of great price. (See Matthew 13:44–46.)

It's time to start releasing faith in the right things. It's time to unite what we have heard with *it*. It's time we come to know the love of Christ, to comprehend its height, length, breadth, and depth. It's time to understand the beauty and simplicity of the good news of the gospel. I was lost. Now I'm found. I was blind. Now I see.

Know the truth about yourself. Know the truth about God. Stop believing the lies.

We can do this. We can believe. We gave ourselves permission to think a certain way and to believe a certain way our whole lives. Let's give ourselves permission to start thinking and believing like heaven.

Put it On

I'd like to borrow an illustration from a dear friend of mine. I heard him one time explain how a lot of Christians treat the gospel like a gift someone receives on Christmas. Let's say for example that I found out that you really wanted a certain jacket and it's something you wanted for a long time. Let's say I bought it for you, wrapped it up all neat and nice, and gave it to you as a surprise. You didn't see it coming. Someone near and dear to you told me you wanted it. Let's say you open it and fall in love with what you see. You're taken aback. You give me a hug and say, "Thank you," remove it from the box, and immediately go hang it up in your closet. You never put it on. It simply takes up closet space. It looks nice on the hanger, but you never received the benefit of it because it never made it across your shoulders.

Theologically, it's not wrong for me to tell you that God loves you. It's not wrong for me to tell you that He forgives you. And I'm not in error when I tell you that He's made you righteous through His once and for all sacrifice. It's one thing to know these things. It's another to receive them and to put them on.

"But as many as received Him, to them He gave the right to become children of God, *even* to those who believe in His name" (John 1:12).

I don't want to just know that God loves me. I want to receive His love. I don't want to know that He forgives me. I want to receive His forgiveness.

I want to put on the wardrobe that Jesus purchased for me.

The truth is that we have what we believe when it comes to the gospel. We are only doing as well as we are believing. Whatever benefit we've derived through it has come by faith. We have to see what it is that Jesus accomplished and say, "Thank you."

Faith Looks Like Something

This book has been written to challenge you to believe the beauty of the things you will read about in the later chapters. It's been written to bring the dead things to life. Remember, if faith comes by *hearing* (Romans 10:17), faith comes through fellowship. I fellowshipped with the wrong things and my life declared it. My fruit bore witness to what it was that I was believing. Your life always reveals what you believe and I've never been more challenged in my life with what it is that I believe than this year, 2013. One thing I learned this year is that faith *looks* like something. There is always evidence for what it is we believe. As you read the next few chapters, you'll be confronted with the same things I was confronted with. You will journey through the very things God had opened my eyes to and it is my hope and prayer that He gives you eyes to see and ears to hear. Indeed, I pray that you begin to unite what it is that you are about to read with faith and are encouraged by the same things that have encouraged me.

I pray that we would discover and put on the beauty of His love and forgiveness.

Be warned: it may appear as if I am repeating myself at times. It is not my intention to fill up pages with useless redundancy. I simply want the realities of what you are reading to be formed in your heart. For that reason, I take the same stance as Paul and Peter. "To write the same things *again* is no trouble to me, and it is a safeguard for you" (Phil. 3:1).

> I will always be ready to remind you of these things, even though you *already* know *them*, and have been established in the truth which is present with *you*. I consider it right, as long as I am in this *earthly* dwelling, to stir you up by way of reminder.
>
> 2 Peter 1:12–13

May what Satan has tried to blind you with through life finally be removed from your eyes. May you come to find what it is you have been looking for your whole life. May you come to see the wonders of His grace through His radical mercy. May we truly come to know the love of Christ. May we see the lovesick Father who never stops looking or His children. May our eyes be forever changed and our bodies flooded with light.

We can see because the light is already shining.

No More Games

Awake, sleeper, And arise from the dead, And Christ will shine on you.

—Ephesians 5:14

Now is the Time

"No more games."

Those were the three words that I believe I had heard in the stillness of my own heart through the Holy Spirit that sparked my journey into what God has been showing me and teaching me throughout the year of 2013. They are the very words that have laid the foundation and framework for everything else you will read about in this book. The very pages you hold in your hand will stretch you and challenge you in the same ways that I have been challenged and stretched this year. They will confront you and encourage you at the same time. And I believe they will cause many to awaken from their slumber and begin to truly believe. Now is *the* time and yet it's always been the time, hasn't it? Jesus would sometimes say things such as "An hour is coming, and now is" in reference to things that were already unfolding in preparation for something that was coming. (See John 4:23 and John 5:25.) God is preparatory in nature.

John the Baptist was always to be the voice of one crying in the wilderness, "Make ready the way of the Lord, make His paths straight." (See Matthew 3:3.) But even he had to prepare in the wilderness to become what he already was. An hour is *coming*, and now *is*.

It was no different with Jesus as well. He was born as the Savior of the world (see John 4:42) but did not begin His ministry until He was thirty years old. (See Luke 3:23). An hour is *coming*, and now *is*.

As Christians, we are people of faith. We come into this thing by faith and we continue to live by it all the days of our lives. (See Ephesians 2:8 and 2 Corinthians 5:7.) We are believers and yet we are always growing, always maturing in the faith until the One who began a good work within us will perfect or complete it when He returns. (See Philippians 1:6.) An hour is *coming*, and now *is*.

Nevertheless, it's *time* to see. It's *time* to believe.

Now more than ever we must learn to live by faith. We must be convinced of what we claim we believe. We must learn to see everything we walk through and go through in this life as an opportunity to manifest the gospel that's been sown in us.

The Good Ole' Boys

Shortly after God had said to me, "No more games," He told me to read the book of Acts. I don't know about you, but there are times when God has asked me to read something that I've already read, and my response can sometimes be, "I already know what that says. Why do I have to read that again?" I took this attitude once when God wanted me to read what many people refer to as the prodigal son story, and thankfully, God met my ignorance with this very statement: "If you take that stance right now, then you're saying that My word never has anything new to say to you." What may have sounded like a rebuke was lifesaving. It was exactly what I needed to hear in that moment, and as it turns out, God had shown me something within that story that I had never seen before! As a result, I was quick to read what He wanted me to read this time around.

The reason that God wanted me to take a look at the book of Acts was unlike any reason that I had read that book before. I remember that when my eyes were opened to the supernatural and that miracles and signs and wonders were still for today, I would read the acts of the disciples and be overwhelmed by how they lived and what they did. But this time, God didn't want me to see that a man was healed at the gate called Beautiful. He didn't want me honing in on all the times that people were filled with the Holy Spirit. He wanted me to see something completely different. He wanted me to see something that was recorded in greater number than all of the miracles that took place through the hands, shadows, and articles of clothing of these boys. He wanted me to see all the times that they were persecuted.

In fact, here is a list of those times:

- Acts 4:1–3 – Peter and John are put in jail.
- Acts 5:17–18 – The high priest puts the apostles in jail.
- Acts 5:40–42 – The apostles are flogged (beaten by a rod or whip).
- Acts 7:58–60 – Stephen is stoned to death.
- Acts 8:1–3 – Saul begins to heavily persecute the church, carrying off men and women from their houses and placing them in jail.
- Acts 9:23–24, 29 – The Jews seek to put Paul to death.
- Acts 12:1–6 – James (the brother of John) is put to death and Peter is placed in prison.
- Acts 13:50 – The Jews incite a persecution against Paul and Barnabas and drive them out of their district.
- Acts 14:4–5 – The Jews and gentiles attempt to mistreat Paul and Barnabas and stone them.
- Acts 14:19 – Paul is stoned, drug out of the city, and left for dead.

- Acts 16:19–25 – Paul and Silas are arrested, beaten with many blows from rods, and thrown into prison.
- Acts 18:4–6 – Paul is rejected and blasphemed against by the Jews.
- Acts 18:12–17 – Sosthenes is beaten before the judgment seat of Gallio.
- Acts 21:27–33 – Paul is seized in the temple by the Jews and placed in chains by the leader of the Roman cohort.
- Acts 23:12–13 – More than forty Jews devise a plot to not eat or drink until they kill Paul.
- Acts 24 – Paul is brought before Felix where accusations are brought against him by the Jews and is left imprisoned for two years.
- Acts 25–26 – Paul is shuffled from Festus to Agrippa while making a defense of his life.
- Acts 27 – Paul is sent to Rome and suffers shipwreck.

As amazing, horrific, and mindblowing as everything they went through is, the way they responded is greater still. Truly, as I read about how the disciples were mistreated and about the injustices that they had faced, I began to realize that God did not want me to be shocked by the very trouble and persecution that has been promised to every believer who seeks to live a life of godliness. (See John 15:20, John 16:33, and 2 Timothy 3:12.) Persecution is a promise. It's not something you get to opt out of. It's called the fellowship of His sufferings. (See Philippians 3:10.) Rather, He wanted me to *see* how they responded. Indeed, there was a strong statement that God was seeking to make, and it was centered and rooted in what these boys believed, because no person in history would have been able to endure what they had endured if they simply believed in a philosophy or a doctrine and did not know the risen Lord, Jesus Christ. You don't suffer for a "belief system." You suffer for a friend.

These guys weren't just baptized in the Spirit to perform signs and wonders. They were also baptized in the Spirit to have the strength, comfort, and boldness to face persecution and walk through trials. We need the power of God to be able to face what they faced. Sometimes, the greatest sign and wonder isn't a miracle. It's a person who walks through the greatest adversities of life and comes out on the other side unchanged and full of joy. It's the ability to walk through fire without smelling like smoke.

The trials that you and I walk through will always reveal what we believe.

> "In this [our imperishable and undefiled inheritance— eternal life!] you greatly rejoice, even though now for a little while, if necessary, you have been distressed by various trials, *so that the proof of your faith, being* more precious than gold which is perishable, even though tested by fire, may be found to result in praise and glory and honor at the revelation of Jesus Christ (emphasis mine).
>
> 1 Peter 1:6–7

You do not get to choose which face you will put on when it comes to trials. There is no "faking it" with them. They reveal what we believe. I can promise you that Paul and Silas and the others were not biting their lips trying to weather the storms they were in. They weren't *trying* to rejoice. Out of the abundance of their hearts, they sang and were willing to take a beating for the good news that set them free. The truth is that we will always see adversity as an opportunity to shine or as an opportunity to whine and the light within these guys had shone brightly in a very dark place.

The evidence of belief is never found in word only. Stating that you believe something that your life doesn't reinforce is in all honesty no belief at all. True believing always bears witness. It always carries with it supporting evidence. It's a mouth backed up by a life lived.

A clear example concerning true believing would look something like this. Let's say a man woke up one particular morning to his alarm. The sound that broke through his clock radio was not the stereotypical *beep, beep, beep, beep* or the sound of sweet music. The first voice this man heard that morning was the voice of a meteorologist reporting the strong possibility of rain that day. After getting out of bed, the man continues along with his morning routine and sits down at the table to a bowl of his favorite cereal for breakfast where he reads the paper every morning. Again, he's made aware of the chance for rain because of what his eyes read concerning the weather.

After breakfast and an invigorating shower, he notices that he has ten minutes to spare before meeting his friend at the local coffee shop. As a result, he spends his next few moments by switching on the television to his favorite news station where they too report about the likelihood of a rainy day. After he switches off his television, he scurries along down Main Street to his meeting. The first thing he announces to his friend after they exchange greetings is, "Looks like it's going to rain today."

His friend, with furrowed brow and all, looks at the man quizzically and says, "You don't believe that."

"Yes, I do," the man argues.

"No, you don't," the friend counters who pulls the umbrella he's carried with him into view. "If you believed that, you'd be carrying one of these."

The point is believing *looks* like something. This is why James penned the famous line that reads "even so faith, if it has no works, is dead, being by itself" (James 2:17). James is not contradicting Paul's doctrinal statement concerning Romans 5:1 where Paul declared that we are justified by faith. No, James is simply saying that faith looks like something. And faith in the case of what the disciples went through is evidenced in how they reacted. In fact, let's take a look at some of those instances to drive this point home.

And now, Lord, take note of their threats, and *grant that Your bond-servants may speak Your word with all confidence,* while You extend Your hand to heal, and signs and wonders take place through the name of Your holy servant Jesus (emphasis mine).

Acts 4:29–30

- This prayer is prayed following the arrest and release of Peter and John.
- They are not asking God to strike their enemies or to remove persecution from them. They are essentially praying for a greater boldness to preach the very thing that just got them into trouble!

They took his [Gamaliel's] advice; and after calling the apostles in, they flogged them and ordered them not to speak in the name of Jesus, and *then* released them. So they went on their way from the presence of the Council, *rejoicing that they had been considered worthy to suffer shame for His name.* And every day, in the temple and from house to house, *they kept right on teaching and preaching Jesus as the Christ* (emphasis mine).

Acts 5:40–42

- They rejoiced for the beating they just took and not only that, they kept right on teaching and preaching the very thing that brought their beating upon them!

Then falling on his knees, he cried out with a loud voice, "*Lord, do not hold this sin against them!*" Having said this, he fell asleep (emphasis mine).

Acts 7:60

- This Stephen had said while in the presence of those who were gnashing their teeth at him and stoning him to death.

On the very night when Herod was about to bring him forward, *Peter was sleeping* between two soldiers, bound with two chains, and guards in front of the door were watching over the prison (emphasis mine).

Acts 12:6

- James, the brother of John, had just been put to death by the sword and because he saw that it pleased the Jews to do so, Herod arrests Peter with the same intent in mind.
- Peter is not freaking out. He's not flustered or is he wondering why this is happening to him. He's asleep, baby! He's completely at peace in the face of the greatest storm he's faced up to this point in his life.

Let's look at one more. I think you're starting to get it.

When they [a crowd from Philippi] had struck them [Paul and Silas] with many blows, they threw them into prison, commanding the jailer to guard them securely; 24and he, having received such a command, threw them into the inner prison and fastened their feet in the stocks. 25*But about midnight Paul and Silas were praying and singing hymns of praise to God*, and the prisoners were listening to them; 26and suddenly there came a great earthquake, so that the foundations of the prison house were shaken; and immediately all the doors were opened and everyone's chains were unfastened (emphasis mine).

Acts 16:23–26

- Paul and Silas are beaten with *many* blows because the masters of a slave-girl, who had a spirit of divination cast out of her, saw that they had lost their opportunity for making profit through fortune-telling.
- Paul and Silas never said this: "I don't know what the deal is, God. It seems like everywhere we go and every time we open our mouths, we are taking a beating. We gave our

lives to You. You'd think the least You could do is watch our backs! Why aren't You protecting us!"

- They didn't say that, did they? No, They sang and they prayed. Why?

Why? That's the question, isn't it? Why?
And how? How did they do it?
The answer is simple: because of what they believed, because of what they had seen and heard. (See Acts 4:20 and 1 John 1:1–3.) I believe that these guys walked around with the consciousness of the following five things (which is by no means an exhaustive list). Truly, it's my belief that these great men of God set their minds on things above and not on the things of the earth (see Colossians 3:2) in this way:

1. They knew that what they were going through was producing something of great value—an eternal weight of glory! (See Romans 5:3–5, Romans 8:18, 2 Corinthians 4:17, James 1:2–4, 1 Peter 1:6–9.)
2. They understood their right standing (righteousness) with God. (See Romans 1:16, Proverbs 28:1.)
3. They had an eternal perspective. They lived for the judgment seat of Christ. (See Hebrews 11:35, 2 Timothy 4:7–8, 2 Corinthians 4:15–5:1.)
4. They understood that their life was not their own. (See Acts 20:24, Galatians 2:20, 1 Corinthians 6:20.)
5. They determined to know nothing but the love of God—Christ and Him crucified. (See 1 Corinthians 2:2, 2 Corinthians 5:14, Ephesians 3:14–19, Philippians 3:7–14.)

The truth is that what we *see* (believe), we will declare with our lives. In John 1:34, John the Baptist, after baptizing Jesus in the Jordan River, says this: "I myself have *seen*, and have *testified* that this is the Son of God" (emphasis mine). Even though faith is the assurance of things hoped for and the conviction of things not seen (see Hebrews 11:1), that assurance and conviction causes you to see. Even though you may not be able to see with your two eyes what you believe, you see it in your heart. You know it to be true! You're assured. You're convinced. And when you are those things, you will declare it with your life! There will be no need for persuasive words of wisdom. The very life you live is the demonstration of what the Spirit is doing in you and of power! (See 1 Corinthians 2:4.)

Connolly, Party of Six

A great example of this is found within the testimony of what my family and I walked out together with the Lord. In November 2012, I was talking with a friend in my office when all of the sudden the following sentence spewed forth from my mouth: "You know, if something were to ever happen to one of my cars, I'd like to believe that I'd have enough faith to trust that God would give me a new one." I don't know why I said it at the time. It just came out. What I didn't understand then, I understand now. I was prophesying over myself a lesson that God wanted me to walk out concerning faith. I was literally declaring a life lesson that would forever change the way I look at the promises of God and the way my family and I would live from that time forward.

Now, before you begin to entertain the thought of me promoting a "prosperity gospel," let me make this point very clear: I am promoting a Father who loves us and knows what we need before we ask Him (Matt. 6:8). I'm not talking about a prosperity gospel. I'm talking about living by faith. I'm not talking about believing a certain way so I can get what I want. I'm talking about a God who tells me to seek first His kingdom and His righteousness and that when I do, all the things that concern me will be added to me (Matt. 6:33). I'm not looking for a genie in a bottle. I've found a Father through whom every good and perfect gift comes (Jas. 1:17).

Ironically, the very next day after the conversation that I had with my friend, I had taken one of my cars to get inspected. A few hours later, I received a phone call from the dealership I had taken my car to explaining that it was going to cost $3,500.00 to fix my car in order for it to pass inspection. Truthfully, this car had been nickeling-and-diming me for the last few years. As a result, I began to wonder if it was worth me fixing it. Thankfully, my best friend suggested that I look to see what the value of the car was on kelleybluebook.com (kbb.com). Wouldn't you know it? The value of the car was identical to the price it would cost me to fix it! Isn't it interesting that this was happening the day after I talked about wanting to believe I'd have enough faith in God if something like this were to go down. And *go down* it was!

After discussing our options with my wife, Nicole, we both decided that the car wasn't worth fixing. In fact, we saw it as an awesome opportunity to manifest faith. I was fully aware of what came out of my mouth the day before, and I was not about to break the word of my oath. Jesus Himself said that we should let our statement be yes-yes or no-no, because anything beyond those is of evil. (See Matthew 5:37.) That's a pretty strong comment!

For the next three months, my family and I were reduced to becoming a one-car household. Can you imagine the madness! We actually had to spend more time together as a family in the same car! What a terrible cross to bear! I hope you are picking up on the sarcasm.

Was it an adjustment at first? Yes. The quality of life and freedom we enjoyed wasn't as strong, but our faith was growing. It's also beneficial to point out that during this interim period of having only one car, my wife and I found out that we were pregnant with what we believed to be our third child in December of 2012 (one month after being reduced to one car). The reason I said that we were pregnant with what we believed to be our third child is because we actually found out we were pregnant with identical twin girls after my wife's ultra sound appointment to verify the pregnancy in January of 2013. It's also significant to point out that there is no history of twins on either side of our family, but like I tell everyone when telling this story, it has to start somewhere!

Do you know what the first thought was that crossed my mind aside from thinking that I'm about to have four girls and things are about to get really crazy really fast? (Don't get me wrong, I love being the father of all girls. In fact, I only ever saw myself with girls). I thought about this: I am so glad I didn't dump $3,500.00 into a car that cannot seat a family of six. Because my children had literally doubled in the matter of one phone call from my wife who was on her way home from her ultra sound appointment, I realized that I no longer needed a car. I needed a minivan and the greatest news and source of comfort for me during that time was found in one verse that I had already referenced above. He [God] knows what I need before I ask Him (Matt. 6:8). I wonder if that's not true. I believed it was.

During our time of waiting, God had blessed us through two families who had each loaned us one of their automobiles to use. The first was through a family at our own church, Praise Community Church in York, PA. This one particular family had loaned us their 2012 Toyota Prius. Man, I loved that car. It was just so neat to drive. My family had the privilege of riding around in it for three months. The only reason the family had to ask for it back was because their son was coming home from the military and needed to use his truck again, which they were driving in his absence.

The funny thing is that I had returned the Prius on a Monday. Two days later, I had received a phone call from a pastor friend of mine who said that he had two vehicles in his church's parking lot that belonged to a family that moved to Mozambique for four months. This particular family left their vehicles behind with strict instructions stating that if anyone was in need of a vehicle, they were to use one of theirs. When did this family leave for Mozambique? The same day I had to return the Prius.

I had enjoyed the Prius until May of 2013. It was two days later that I received a GMC Envoy in the same month from the family who left to study to become missionaries at the Harvest School in Pemba, Mozambique. Because they were gone for four months; that meant I could use the Envoy until the end of August. The twins were due September 25, but they decided to make an early appearance. Because my wife had developed preeclampsia with severe headaches, the girls were born premature seven weeks early on Saturday, August 10. They were delivered cesarean in consideration of my wife's health.

Never did I anticipate the girls being born before the arrival of the minivan. I didn't know how God was going to do it before, and I certainly didn't know how He was going to do it now! In fact, I used to joke with my congregation and say, "I don't know how He's going to do it. I just believe He's going to. I'm not sure if you are organizing a secret fundraiser behind my back or if someone is going to drive by my house one day and pull in the driveway because they "feel" like they are supposed to give me their van, or if He's going to make it appear out of the thin air. All I know is that He said He knows what I need before I ask Him." And that's all I needed to know.

Three days after the twins were born, I received this very e-mail while in the NICU visiting my little preemies:

Dear Brian,

Congratulations on the birth of your twins!

Several weeks ago I attended a service at Praise where you gave the message. In the service you mentioned the need of a van. I believe God began speaking to me that my husband and I need to contribute to that need. After much prayer, we believe it is God's desire for us to purchase a van for you. My husband has been looking online and found some great selections, but we feel that you should be a part of the decision. It is our desire that God be given the glory and our names not be known by others.

One of the awesome privileges I have is to travel and share the gospel with people. During 2013, I would often share about my wife and I waiting and believing God for a van. I would *never* share about our journey of faith in hopes to elicit sympathy from people so that someone might buy us one. I never talked about it in a way that was manipulative and tried to play on the heart strings of people so that they would feel sorry for my wife and I. No. I was trying to make a point. I was seeking to demonstrate that He who promised is faithful (see Hebrews 10:23) and that it was my desire for everyone who knew me to see the salvation of God in my life.

What's so neat about this woman's e-mail is that she said that she "attended a service at Praise where I gave the message." It's important to point out that this woman doesn't attend my church. It's also important to say that I might share the message on Sunday morning once a month. So here is a woman who doesn't attend my church who just so happened to attend a Sunday morning service that I just so happened to be speaking at.

The truth is, I didn't want anyone from my church to buy me a minivan. I didn't want anyone in my family to buy us one either. That's too close to home. That's too easy. That's all but expected. The fact that this was a stranger who just so happened to hear me talking about the birth of my twins and waiting on the promises of God made this event all the more miraculous.

The long story short is this: This woman and her husband purchased my family a 2012 Toyota Sienna LE with 10,600 miles on it for $27,500.00. Why? He knows what I need before I ask Him, and He knew I needed a vehicle that would seat a family of six. He does it because He loves. He does it because He's good and He knows how to care for His children and He knows how to flow through His children. I am so thankful that this couple heard the voice of God and obeyed. It still amazes me. And yet as I drove the van off the dealership's lot, I thought I'd be more excited than I was. I actually felt guilty that I wasn't pounding the steering wheel and screaming at the top of my lungs. But the reason why I wasn't reacting that way had to do with what I *saw* the whole time while waiting for God to fulfill His promise to my family. The truth is I had always seen His provision because I saw it in His word and I united it with faith. As I was driving away, I thought (and I hope this doesn't sound arrogant), "*Yep. That's just what He does.*"

Was I shocked that the twins were born before the minivan was parked in my driveway? Yes. Truthfully, the closer it got to the twins' due date, the easier it was to entertain thoughts about finding other alternatives to purchase a minivan. But why settle for an Ishmael when you can have an Isaac? And as I said before, I did not want to break the word of my oath. I wanted to see the fruit of what I claimed I believed. And one of the things I learned during this amazing lesson was this: It's not about the waiting. It's about the promise.

Humbled

If faith can be released into something as small as trusting God to provide for our families (which may not seem like a small thing), what would happen if we believed the *whole* thing? What if we began to truly believe the gospel? What if we truly believed that God loved us, that He forgave us, that He redeemed us, that He reconciled us, that He saved us? You might say at this point, "That's blasphemous! Of course, I believe those things! How dare you propose that I don't believe the gospel!" I understand that we believe to a degree. I understand that we are growing in things. And I am in no way trying to suggest that anyone reading this is completely void of faith. All I am saying is that those guys in the book of Acts went through what they went through willingly with joy, never wondering where God was or why He was allowing it to happen and the majority of Christians are falling apart because Sister Susie or Brother Willie didn't call them back on the phone. It's got to be more than that!

One of the most humbling things God revealed to me this year is found in Hebrews 11, what most people commonly refer to as *the faith chapter*. Although there are numerous pillars of faith recorded in this particular section of scripture, God didn't want me to see those listed by name. He wanted me to see the nameless ones.

> And what more shall I say? For time will fail me if I tell of Gideon, Barak, Samson, Jephthah, of David and Samuel and the prophets, *who by faith conquered kingdoms, performed acts of righteousness, obtained promises, shut the mouths of lions, quenched the power of fire, escaped the edge of the sword, from weakness were made strong, became mighty in war, put foreign armies to flight. Women received back their dead by resurrection; and others were tortured, not accepting their release, so that they might obtain a better resurrection; and others experienced mockings and scourgings, yes, also chains and imprisonment. They were stoned, they were sawn in two, they were tempted, they were put to death with the sword; they went about in sheepskins, in goatskins, being destitute, afflicted, ill-treated [men of whom the world was not worthy], wandering in deserts and mountains and caves and holes in the ground.* And all these, having gained approval through their faith, did not receive what was promised, because God had provided something better for us, so that apart from us they would not be made perfect (emphasis mine).

> Hebrews 11:32–40

Do you want to know what the truth is? These men and women did what they did without a Bible. They didn't have a pastor or preacher to listen to every Sunday morning. They weren't seminary trained. They didn't have access to countless books or teachings on mp3. They weren't able to watch their favorite minister on YouTube. They did what they did because they united what they heard with faith. What's all the more amazing is contained in the last two verses listed above. These men and women did what they did without receiving the promise that we've received—Christ Jesus, the Lord. These men and women were not Spirit-filled, born-again believers. They were not possessors of the new covenant where sins are remembered no more. No. They *believed*. If they could do what they did without the promise, what's possible *now* for those of us who would finally awaken to what we have received? This is why I say, "What if we began to truly believe the gospel?"

Would you like to hear a sobering thought? We are *all* going to stand before the judgment seat of Christ so that each and every one of us may be recompensed (rewarded, compensated, repaid, or reimbursed) for the things we did while on the earth, whether good or bad. (See 2 Corinthians 5:10). *We are all going to stand*; that means even those above listed in Hebrews 11, that means people like John Wesley, Martin Luther, Charles Finney, George Whitefield, Kathryn Kuhlman, Smith Wigglesworth, John G. Lake, and the like. I couldn't imagine rubbing shoulders with these amazing men and women of the faith and say with my mouth that I believed what they believed. If I'm not living what they lived, I never believed it, but I *want* to. Don't be deceived. It's time to wake up. Let's stop learning and start living.

Indeed, we will forever live out what we understand and there's something about understanding the radical love, mercy, grace, and forgiveness of the cross that radically transforms your life. Those boys listed above in the book of Acts believed the gospel! Those talked about in Hebrews 11 had faith! The disciples believed that Jesus was the fulfillment of everything they were waiting for. They believed that they were made new. They believed that there is an inheritance that's imperishable and undefiled and will not fade away waiting for them in heaven—eternal life! (1 Peter 1:4). They believed they were loved and accepted. They believed that they were forgiven. They believed that God wanted them and that He came to seek and to save them.

The goal of this book is really quite simple—that we'd believe, that we'd believe the beauty and simplicity of the gospel and wake up. Indeed, my hope is that we would see that He is everything we've been looking for and that we are forgiven. It's my conviction that the strength of the disciples' lives came out of the revelation that God is for them and that nothing could separate them from the love of Christ. (See Romans 8:32, 35–39.) Nothing can separate us from the love of Christ because sin has been dealt with once and for all. (See Hebrews 10:12.) You are forgiven. This is where confidence and boldness stems from. This is what causes a man who had denied Jesus three times to take his stand with the eleven and raise his voice bringing a charge against his hearers that they killed the very Messiah they had been waiting for their whole lives. (See Acts 2:14, 23.) This is what causes these same three thousand hearers to be saved. (See Acts 2:41.) This is what caused a man from Lystra who had been lame from his mother's womb to have faith to be healed. (See Acts 14:9.) This is the very gospel that Paul preached.

> Let it be known to you, brethren, that *through Him (Jesus) forgiveness of sins is proclaimed to you*, and *through Him everyone who believes is freed from all things*, from which you could not be freed through the Law of Moses (emphasis mine).
>
> Acts 13:38–39

This is the very gospel Jesus told us to proclaim.

> Then He opened their (the disciples) minds to understand the Scriptures, and He said to them, "Thus it is written, that the Christ would suffer and rise again from the dead the third day, and *that repentance for forgiveness of sins would be proclaimed in His name to all the nations, beginning from Jerusalem.*
>
> Luke 24:45–47

Truly, it's this gospel that signs and wonders will follow. "And they went out and preached everywhere, while the Lord worked with them, and confirmed the word by the signs that followed" (Mark 16:20).

It's time to unite what we have heard with faith and to declare it with our lives.

No more games.

It's time to see. It's time to believe.

It's time to wake up, because the light is already shining.

"Awake, sleeper, And arise from the dead, And Christ will shine on you" (Eph. 5:14).

Who's Looking for Whom?

For the Son of Man has come to seek and to save that which was lost.

—Luke 19:10

I Once Was Lost, but Now I'm Found

Have you ever been lost?

I mean have you ever been really, really, really lost? It has to be one of the scariest moments in a person's life.

"I have no idea where I am."　　　*"What if no one finds me?"*
"Will I ever find my way out?"　　*"Will I ever see anyone again?"*
"What if I'm stuck here forever?"

Adrenaline begins to course through your veins as if you're hooked directly to an IV drip. The whole fight or flight thing kicks in and you instantly find yourself in survival mode. In fact, perhaps the "Eye of the Tiger" by Survivor begins to play in your mind. You know, Rocky III? "It's the eye of the tiger. It's the thrill of the fight?"

Anyway, maybe you begin to wish that you paid a little closer attention to MacGyver when he was on television. Either way, you know deep down that there is no amount of duct tape that can get you out of this jam.

You have only one goal in mind: *I need to find my way back.*

Back where?

Where did you come from?

Where are you going back to?

And better yet, how do you know *when* you're no longer *lost?*

When I was about to begin the adventure that is being a freshman in high school, which more than likely dated me at fourteen or fifteen years of age at that time, my family and I had taken a vacation to tour the states of Colorado, Utah, and Arizona. My father has always been an avid camper, and this particular trip was no different. He had it worked out that by the time our airplane touched down in Denver; we immediately made our way to our new home for the next two weeks—an RV. We slept, we ate, and we went to the bathroom in this RV. We did life together in this RV, and it was fun. In fact, one of my fondest memories as silly as this might sound, was waking up in the morning to the cool Colorado air and eating a bowl of Fruity Pebbles in the stillness of the mountainous terrain.

Eating Fruity Pebbles wasn't the only thing that we did, however. We rode horses. We explored tourist attractions. We played board games. We made new friends.

And we went hiking.

Although I am unable to recall everything that took place during our hike up this particular mountain, I am fully capable of remembering all that took place during my descent. For some reason unbeknownst to me to this day, my stepbrother Josh and I decided to venture off on our own away from the rest of the family in hopes to beat them down the mountain back to the RV. What was supposed to be a "shortcut" down turned out to be a "detour" that led us around and around and around.

To say that fear was slowly creeping in would have been an understatement. I was terrified. What used to be a visible path that had been worn down by the many steps of pedestrians had suddenly been swallowed up by wildlife. We were no longer on the "beaten path." We were blazing a new one. During this time, very few words were exchanged between my stepbrother and me. Our silence said it all. We wanted to find what we were looking for. We wanted to be reunited with our family. We wanted to be back *home*.

Although shrubs and trees and bushes covered the mountain side and limited our visibility, we at least had enough common sense to keep making our way down. We thought that if we could at least make it to the base of the mountain, we would be able to wander around the bottom until we identified the parking lot where the RV resided. Truthfully, it seemed as if we would never find our way back, though. Everything appeared to be unfamiliar. And the more unfamiliar our surroundings became, the louder the voice in my head shouted, "You'll never find your way back."

With our hearts nearly pounding out of our chest due to the anxiety of the moment, we finally made our way onto level ground. With our footing firm, we looked around and realized that we just so happened to stumble upon our parking lot. As beautiful as the sight of that RV looked at that moment for our sore eyes, the sound of our family's voices were sweeter still. We were home. We were safe. And the joy we experienced in that moment was synonymous with what it was that we had found.

My entire life before Christ is truthfully no different than what it was that I had experienced, felt, and walked through while lost in the mountains of Colorado. I was sincerely one of the most *lost* people you would have ever met. I stumbled. I fell. I groped. I searched. I did all of those things in darkness. I couldn't see. I was so blinded by my own pain and the lies I had believed for the majority of my life.

I gave myself to things. If it was an addiction, I tried it. Food. Approval. Lying. Performance. Pornography. Drugs. I thought all of it was the answer, but all it could offer was *passing pleasure*. The satisfaction was fleeting. It never remained. The things I did would leave me hungrier and thirstier than when I started and the more I grew accustomed to them, the more I needed from them and the more I needed to use them. The ante would always go up. Five compliments weren't enough. I needed ten. Marijuana wasn't enough. I needed crack cocaine. Pornographic pictures weren't enough. I needed to watch videos. Succeeding at a few things wasn't enough. I needed to do well at everything.

The truth is that everything I thought was the answer ultimately revealed what it was that I was looking for. *You know you're lost because you keep searching.* You live like a vampire bleeding everything dry only to find out that the life you drained from whatever you thought was the answer could never give you life.

You know you're found when you stop searching.

My search ended at nineteen years of age on a cool November evening in the living room of my house in Gilbertsville, PA. After years and years of destructive behavior toward myself and others, I had finally come to an end in and of myself. Approximately one month prior to this night, I had a near overdose experience with crack cocaine. The result was that I spent every moment of every day of that following month believing that I had done so much damage to my heart over the years of drug use and being overweight that I was experiencing heart attack type symptoms. There was a constant pain within my chest centering over where my heart was located.

After eating, sleeping, and living with that fear for thirty days, I decided to bring my plight before my mother. I can still see the scene I'm about to describe to you as clear as day in my mind just as if it happened yesterday. As I made my way into the living room, I saw my mom sitting in the far right corner on my brother's favorite blue chair. It was the chair he would fall asleep on almost every day after school while growing up. The room was still. The television was turned off. We had no overhead lights, so the only light that filled the room radiated from underneath and above the shades that covered our lamps. The couch I was about to sit in sat across from my mom, centered neatly against the left wall. I took my seat and began this life altering moment with these words: "Mom, I need to tell you something." And tell her something I did!

I explained to her everything that I had been doing and was involved in for the last few years. She heard every ugly secret I had been hiding. I explained to her what had happened to me the month prior concerning my brush with death over the use of crack cocaine and all she did was look at me—lovingly. There was peace in her eyes. Her face was full of compassion. She didn't revile me and spew the things many of us are so used to hearing: "I can't believe you did that! You know better than that! Do you have any idea how much you've hurt me? You've ruined everyone's life around you!" No such words were found in her mouth, on her tongue, nor worn on her face. In fact, what was seen in her eyes and posture was everything I was looking for. There was grace. There was forgiveness. There was love. There was acceptance.

I was not prepared for what it was that my mom was about to say or what it was that she was about to do. She simply asked, "Can I show you something?" Believe me, when you're in the kind of state that I was in, you're ready to try or be shown anything! What else do you have? What other choice could you possibly make? You're at the end of your rope. You can't climb down any further. The only thing to do is climb back up!

"Sure, Mom," I said.

She puts a VHS tape into the VCR. When she hits the play button, the first thing that appears on the television is a bald man dressed in a black suit. He had a red beard and I swear to you that it looked as if he was shining! Now, it could have been the light of the room reflecting off his freshly polished bald head, but I like to think that something or *someone else* was shining around him. This bald man with a black suit and red beard was lifting his eyes upward and singing into a microphone about how the blood of Jesus covered his sins. He was singing about forgiveness. He was singing about love. And He was putting music to the very thing I knew I needed.

What happened next, I can't explain. The levy broke. No one asked me if I were to die today where I would go. No one asked me to pray a prayer with them. No one talked to me about my sins. All I know is that what that man was singing about, I needed, and as I listened to his words, I cried profusely, and God healed the pain that was in my chest and broke the addictions I had to drugs and cigarettes in one moment of time. Through the tears, I gave myself to Him. I realized that He was everything I was looking for my entire life. And I was introduced to the One who loved me and forgave me by a bald headed man with a black suit and a red beard and a mother who didn't hold my sins against me but had always believed the best about me. I was her son, and for the first time in my life, I felt like I was found. I was home.

The Kingdom of God Is Like...

Throughout Matthew 13, Jesus would use natural illustrations (parables) to explain what the kingdom of heaven is like. He compares it to a man who sowed good seed in his field only to have an enemy sow tares among what he had already sown—wheat. (See Matthew 13:24–30.) He compares it to a mustard seed that a man sowed in his field that eventually became the largest tree where the birds of the air nest in its branches. (See Matthew 13:31–32.) He compares it to leaven. (See Matthew 13:33–34.) Jesus not only gives us an understanding of what the kingdom of heaven is like and how it operates; He also reveals the very heartbeat of heaven and reveals why it is that He had come.

In Matthew 13:44, we read, "The kingdom of heaven is like a treasure hidden in the field, which a man found and hid *again*; and from joy over it he goes and sells all that he has and buys that field."

And in Matthew 13:45–46, we read "Again, the kingdom of heaven is like a merchant seeking fine pearls, and upon finding one pearl of great value, he went and sold all that he had and bought it."

I'd like to propose to you, dear reader, that Jesus is the man who for the joy of what He found, went, and sold all He had to purchase the field so that He might obtain the treasure hidden within it. I'd like to propose to you, dear reader, that Jesus is the merchant seeking fine pearls, and upon finding one of great value, He went and sold all that He had and bought it. I'd also like to propose to you, dear reader, that you are that treasure. You are that one pearl of great price. It's imperative that we understand that this is how God feels about us. We must see what it is that He sees about us. We must comprehend that when it comes to God and His pursuit of man, there is no rock He will leave unturned to find us. He is *relentless* in all that He does and there is great joy in what it is that He finds. For some reason, the streets of gold in heaven (see Revelation 21:21) and the worship of the four living creatures and twenty-four elders (see Revelation 4:8-11) and the rest of the angelic host doesn't cut it. It's not enough for Him. He still wants us. Heaven wouldn't be the same without us. We were in His heart from the beginning.

> Blessed *be* the God and Father of our Lord Jesus Christ, who has blessed us with every spiritual blessing in the heavenly *places* in Christ, just as *He chose us in Him before the foundation of the world*, that we would be holy and blameless before Him. *In love He predestined us to adoption as sons through Jesus Christ to Himself*, according to the kind intention of His will (emphasis mine).
>
> Ephesians 1:3–5

Joy, Joy, Joy

Hebrews 12:2 explains that for the joy set before Jesus, He endured the cross. In other words, He was willing to go through the greatest injustice in human history because of what waited for Him on the other side of being marred (disfigured) more than any other man. (See Isaiah 52:14.) But the question is, what in fact was the joy that was set before Him? I suppose an argument could be made that the joy that was set before Jesus was being exalted to His father's right hand (see Acts 2:33) or that He accomplished the will of the Father (see Hebrews 10:9) or that He would offer one sacrifice for sins for all time (see Hebrews 10:12). These would all be plausible reasons for Jesus's joy, and yet I'd like to suggest based on the scriptures from Matthew 13 above that you were the joy that was set before Him. I believe it brought Jesus great pleasure knowing that He would be the first-born among many brethren. (See Romans 8:29.) I believe Jesus took great delight in knowing that because of His one act of righteousness the result would be justification of life to all men and that through His obedience many would be made righteous. (See Romans 5:18–19.) In other words, I believe that Jesus was pretty pumped to see the Father's children, His very brothers and sisters, be set free in order to come back home, in order to one day partake of the very place He has gone to prepare for us. (See John 14:2.)

Truly, the Father sent His son into the world to proclaim the greatest news that would ever befall upon the human ear. "God, after He spoke long ago to the fathers in the prophets in many portions and in many ways, in these last days *has spoken to us in His Son*, whom He appointed heir of all things, through whom also He made the world" (Heb. 1:1–2).

Through the Son, the Father shouts to all His children to come home.

Through the Son, the Father screams that repentance for forgiveness of sins is offered. (See Luke 24:47.)

Through the Son, the Father cries, "I love you." (See John 3:16, 1 John 4:10, John 15:13, Romans 5:8.)

Through the Son, the Father declares peace between us and Himself and that those who were once enemies have now become friends. (See Romans 5:1 and Colossians 1:20.)

Through the Son, the Father declares that you are accepted. (See Romans 15:7.)

Through the Son, the Father pronounces you to be a new creature because old things have passed away and new things have come. (See 2 Corinthians 5:17.)

Through the Son, you are presented to the Father as holy, blameless and beyond reproach. (See Colossians 1:22.)

Through the Son, we are dead to sin but alive to the Father. (See Romans 6:11.)

Through the Son the Father whispers to us that we are His children. (See John 1:12 and 1 John 3:1.)

All of these things and more the Father has spoken to us through His son. Not only has the Father spoken these things through Jesus; He has also revealed who He is and what He is like to us.

"He [Jesus] is the radiance of His glory and the *exact representation of His nature*" (Heb. 1:3; emphasis mine).

Heaven Goes Bankrupt

Luke 19:10 states that Jesus came to *seek* and to *save* that which was *lost*. In fact, there were many reasons why Jesus came:

- To preach the kingdom of God (Luke 4:43)
- To testify to the truth (John 18:37)
- To destroy the works of the devil (1 John 3:8)
- To give us life and to have it abundantly (John 10:10)
- To save the world (John 3:16)

As great and as many are the reasons for the Father sending His son, I believe that Luke 19:10 embodies them all. He came to seek and save that which was lost by destroying the works of the devil, giving us life, testifying to the truth, preaching the kingdom of God, and by saving the world. Indeed, after Jesus had been led into the wilderness by the Spirit to be tempted by Satan, He returned to Galilee in the power of the Spirit and began to preach and say, "Repent, for the kingdom of heaven is at hand."

(See Matthew 4:23.) Although there is much to say on this one verse alone, let me say this: Jesus revealed that the kingdom of heaven looks like a father who is desperately searching to find his lost children and there is no child too lost for Him to find, no place too far that he wouldn't go, and nothing too difficult that He can't overcome. We know this to be true simply because of the exchange of these words between Jesus and Philip found in John 14:8–9.

> Philip said to Him, "Lord, show us the Father, and it is enough for us." Jesus said to him, "Have I been so long with you, and *yet* you have not come to know Me, Philip? He who has seen Me has seen the Father; how *can* you say, "Show us the Father"?

Everything that Jesus said and did revealed the heart of the Father. He was the image of the invisible God. (See Colossians 1:15), and He has explained who and what the Father is like. (See John 1:18.)

Through Jesus's life and death, we are confronted with the fact that heaven spent all that it had in order to obtain who we are. First Corinthians 6:20 says that we were bought with a price. God purchased us through the tearing of His own flesh and the shedding of His own blood. My best friend, Pastor Adam Bower, says it best. "The only thing worth more in the economy of God than the blood of His own Son is your life." Indeed, heaven, for one moment in time, went bankrupt in order to purchase us, the pearl of great price—the treasure hidden in the field! And now what heaven spent is being replenished with interest through every soul that says yes to what it paid for.

In fact, our value to God is found within the mathematics of heaven. One thing is for sure, numbers never lie. They are the measuring stick for everything in this life (temperature, bank accounts, attendance, grade point average, size, weight, etc.) and it's no different when it comes to how God measures your value.

The clearest example of this is found in Luke 15. In this chapter, Jesus refers to a shepherd who leaves ninety-nine sheep in the open pasture to find one that is lost and a woman who goes bananas searching for one lost silver coin when she still has nine left. Let's look at these specific verses together:

> What man among you, if he has a hundred sheep and has lost one of them, does not leave the ninety-nine in the open pasture and go after the one which is lost until he finds it? When he has found it, he lays it on his shoulders, rejoicing. And when he comes home, he calls together his friends and his neighbors, saying to them, "Rejoice with me, for I have found my sheep which was lost!"
>
> Luke 15:4–6

> Or what woman, if she has ten silver coins and loses one coin, does not light a lamp and sweep the house and search carefully until she finds it? When she has found it, she calls together her friends and neighbors, saying, "Rejoice with me, for I have found the coin which I had lost!"
>
> Luke 15:8–9

Truly, there are several things to glean from these two parables. The first thing I'd like to point out is Jesus is extremely personal. We must see ourselves as the "one." There was *one* lost sheep. There was *one* lost coin.

The second thing is Jesus doesn't stop looking for you until He finds you. In fact, some people might call His methods foolish. He seems to be risking what He already has an abundance of in order to find one person. Now let's stop and think about this for a moment. Let's say that you have $100 and you realize that $1 is missing. That means you still have $99. What's $1 in comparison to $99? What the shepherd in the parable does by leaving ninety-nine sheep in the open pasture to find the one that was lost would be like you leaving your $99 out in the open around a bunch of people who have a reputation for stealing so that you can find the $1 that's lost solely because deep down you believe that the other $99 isn't complete without the one that's missing. Why would Jesus do such a thing? Because He doesn't want to imagine life without you. You're a part of the family portrait! Your life has value!

The third thing is Jesus (and all of heaven for that matter) gets really pumped when He finds what He's been looking for. Picture this with me. Jesus compares how the Father feels when one sinner repents to the giddiness of a housewife who finds *one* coin after turning her house upside down in search of it. Think about it. One coin. This one coin is so *valuable*, so *important* to this woman that she calls her friends and neighbors to come and rejoice with her over what it was that she found! One coin! Come on! If someone called me and said, "Hey, Brian, you need to come over! We need to party! I had ten quarters and lost one, but I searched for hours and hours and you'll never believe it, but I found it!" Honestly, I'd think, *Buddy, you need to get a grip! It was one quarter!* What seems insignificant to us means everything to God.

He's *personal*. He's *persistent*. And He *knows how to party!*

Whereas God appears to be relentlessly searching for us in the two parables mentioned above, He sometimes searches by *watching* and *waiting*. The third parable found in Luke 15 communicates this beautifully. Most of us are familiar with the story about a father who has two children. The youngest son approaches his father and asks his dad for his share of the inheritance. Upon receiving his share from his father, the youngest son takes what was given to him and squanders it on what the Bible calls loose-living. (See Luke 15:13.) We read later in the same chapter that loose-living was a polite way of saying that the younger brother wasted his money on prostitutes. (See Luke 15:30.)

The bottom line is we have all at some point in time spent our lives on things that didn't satisfy in search of the One that is the bread of life. (See John 6:48.) We may not have been spending money on prostitutes, but we gave ourselves to something else other than the glory of God. Our whole life apart from God was me-focused. It was about what we wanted, what we thought was the answer, and what we believed was the way to think and live. We spent the very life God had given to us on ourselves while all the while looking for the life that can only come from Him. And the whole time we were doing that, He never lost sight of who we were.

How do we know this? Because He never treated us according to our sins. (See Psalm 103:10.) Now if He is not weighing people by the mistakes they've made and by how they've missed the mark, then He must be measuring them by a different standard. He must be seeing us through a different eye. I believe 2 Corinthians 5:14 reveals the measuring stick of God. Apostle Paul writes that *one* (Jesus) died for all. The once and for all sacrifice of Christ reveals how God sees us and how He feels about us. Truly, God revealed through that one act that took place two thousand years ago on the hill of Golgotha that all men and all women are worthy to drink and eat of the price Jesus paid for them. He didn't purchase trash. He purchased what was of great value to Him.

How God sees us is no different than how I would see my girls if they left home and gave themselves to the most horrific things that human imagination could conjure up. I'm the father of four beautiful girls, and I can promise you that there is nothing that they could do that could cause me to see them any less than how I see them in my heart. Even if my natural eyes saw them stripping at a club or prostituting on a street corner, my heart would see the children I once held in my arms and sang to at night. They would never *not* be daddy's little girl. And there is nothing that they could do that would cause me to stop looking for them or to stop waiting for them. Why? Because I'd know who they are even if they couldn't see who they are.

Hebrews 4:3 states that God rested from His works before the foundation of the world, and Isaiah 46:10 says that He declares the end from the beginning. I often teach people that He knew what He was going to have to do from the beginning and it never changed His mind concerning us. He knew He would have to send His Son to die on our behalf because it's too important to Him that we'd live. We were chosen from the foundation of the world to be found in Him holy and blameless. (See Ephesians 1:4.) He knew that the only way that such a statement would become a reality would be through the greatest injustice any man would ever suffer. Not only that, He knew every lie I'd ever tell, everything I'd ever steal, every person I'd ever hurt, every drug I'd ever take, every x-rated act I'd ever commit, and He still said, "Let there be." He still brought me into existence knowing full well the mess I'd make, because He's not threatened by the mess. He's the Lamb of God who takes away the sin of the world (see John 1:29), not the Lamb of God who exposes the sin of the world.

This is why the father with the two sons in Luke 15 can wait for his son's return. This is why he rejects his son's well rehearsed speech about sinning and not being worthy to be called his son. This is why the father can call for the ring and the robe and the sandals. This is why the father can order the killing of the fattened calf. He never saw the son that left. He saw the son who was always in his heart. And when his son couldn't run to him because of the shame his son was carrying, he ran to him.

Why? Because in the midst of his waiting and watching, he found the son that never left his heart. Even though his son's feet carried the son off to a distant land, he never lost sight of who his son was.

I believe that this was also the case in the beginning in a little known paradise called the garden of Eden. Even though I have already referenced some of these things in the introduction, I'd like to build upon what I have already said. Immediately after Adam and Eve had eaten from the tree of the knowledge of good and evil, the Bible tells us that their eyes were opened and that they knew that they were naked. They had also sewn fig leaves together and made themselves loin coverings. (See Genesis 3:7.) The glory that once clothed them and the breath of life that was once breathed into them had escaped them. Truly, in that one act of disobedience, they had lost the image that they were once created in. What Satan had suggested to Eve through the eating of the tree actually had the opposite effect. She didn't become like God. She lost what she already was.

As a result of their transgression, the wrong sets of eyes were opened. Rather than seeing themselves through their Father's eyes and heart, they weighed themselves for what they did wrong. They saw their mistake and the fear of punishment crept in. They were instantly made aware of their blunder and hid themselves among the trees of the garden. The sound of the Lord walking in the garden in the cool of the day that once brought them comfort and security now became the sound of terror for them. (See Genesis 3:8.)

What happens next is truly quite fascinating. The reaction that Adam and Eve were anticipating from God the Father was not the reaction that they received. They were ready to be punished. They were set to be scorned through a look of disappointment. They were prepared to get what they deserved. They were awaiting an earful of ridicule. But none of that happened. Instead, the story continues this way in Genesis 3:9. "Then the LORD God called to the man, and said to him, '*Where are you?*'" (emphasis mine)."

"Where are you?" *not* "What did you do? How could you have done this? I gave you everything, Adam, and this is how you treat Me? I asked you to do one thing, just *one thing*, and you couldn't even do that!" No such words came forth from God's mouth. He wasn't interested in punishing. He was concerned about restoring what was now lost.

God asked where Adam was because Adam was hiding. We are immediately confronted with a God who has come to *seek* and *save* that which was *lost*. Adam is hiding. God is seeking. What's God looking for? His children. What is He saving?

Everything that we lost. What was lost? Our identity. Our purpose. Our image. Our relationship with God, one another, and creation itself. Our very soul.

Musician and founder of Fire Rain Ministries, Rick Pino,[1] sums this idea up well by having said the following one day in the form of a post on Facebook: "How GREAT is God's love for humanity! 1/3 of His angels fall and He doesn't seem to flinch… Two humans fall and He takes on our frame forever!"

Ever since the fall man has been in hiding and God has been seeking. We've hidden behind wrong thinking, wrong believing, and wrong living. And yet at the same time, everything that we've been hiding behind reveals the very person we've been looking for. What we thought was the answer points to the insatiable search to find our way back into the arms of our Father.

The Other Side of the Coin

It's truly imperative to understand that God would stop it nothing to find His children. He sent His only begotten Son to get the job done. It's just as important, however, to understand that He is everything we've ever been looking for. It's imperative that we grasp the fact that because He came to seek and to save that which was lost, we can stop looking for what it is that He has found—ourselves.

John 1:4 states that in Him (Jesus) was life, and the life was the light of men. That simply means that the light comes on through Jesus Christ. I can know who I am and why I am because of Him. I can know who God is and why God is through Jesus Christ as well. You can only see when the light is shining. Fellowship with the light results in illumination. I can see the truth about my value and identity through Him. I can see the truth about the Father and who He really is through Jesus. I can also see the truth about every single person on the planet through Him as well. The truth is that Jesus died for everyone and as a result, I no longer have to weigh anyone by face value, a book by its cover.

(See 2 Corinthians 5:14–16.) They are loved by God and He paid a price for them.

Life is in Him. You come alive through Him. If anything less than Jesus is the answer, it will always be the problem. The opinion of man can never be the answer. Your performance can never be the answer. As long as a person can only feel good about who they are when people are singing their praise or when they are performing optimally, they will be destroyed when those things aren't flowing. The extreme buzz they feel from everyone's approval and their own success will be equally matched by the hangover they feel through a person's rejection and their own failure.

There has to be a better way to live.

The truth is that we were never created to find ourselves through such things. Acts 17:24–28 make this point abundantly clear by saying this:

> The God who made the world and all things in it, since He is Lord of heaven and earth, does not dwell in temples made with hands; nor is He served by human hands, as though He needed anything, since *He Himself gives to all people life and breath and all things*; and He made from one *man* every nation of mankind to live on all the face of the earth, having determined *their* appointed times and the boundaries of their habitation, *that they would seek God, if perhaps they might grope for Him and find Him*, though He is not far from each one of us; *for in Him we live and move and exist*, as even some of your own poets have said, "For we also are His children" (emphasis mine).

He's the giver of life. Significance and purpose is found in Him, and it's His great desire that we would find all that we are looking for in Him to the point of reaching, groping, and feeling for it because He is not far from each of us.

To every person who has ever discovered His love and grace and to every person who has yet to taste and see that He is good, (See Psalm 34:8.) He is the object of our desire. He is the treasure. He is the pearl. When we understand this, when we finally realize that He is the end of every search, whether it'd be for love, acceptance, forgiveness, mercy, grace, or significance, we will sell everything we have in order to obtain all that He offers and all that He is.

How do you sell everything you have in order to purchase what heaven gives? The answer is found in Jesus's very words. "If anyone wishes to come after Me, he must deny himself, and take up his cross and follow Me" (Matt. 16:24). You give up all that you acquired through sin and the fall of man and say yes to all that He is. You recognize that you were never created to live the way life taught you to live. Jesus Himself said that we have only one teacher. (See Matthew 23:8.) You see who you were created to be through Jesus because He says, "Follow Me" (see Mark 1:17) and you begin to be transformed by the renewing of your mind. (See Romans 12:2.) The way that seems right to a man (see Proverbs 14:12) is replaced with the wisdom of heaven found through the life of Jesus Christ.

The following are some of the questions that this book seeks to answer:

- Do we truly understand what it is that we have found (or if you haven't yet found it, what it is that you are looking for)?
- Do we fully know who it is that has found us (or if you're not yet found, who is looking for you)?
- In other words, have we united faith with the good news we have heard? Are some of us living like the Israelites who likewise had good news preached to them but did not profit from it because they did not release faith in what they heard? (See Hebrews 4:2.) Are we living like the man David describes in Psalm 32:1 that reads, "How blessed is the man whose transgression is forgiven, whose sin is

covered"? Or are we like David in Psalm 51:12 who is asking God to restore to him the joy of His salvation? Do we really believe the things found in Psalm 103:1–13.

Bless the LORD, O my soul, And all that is within me, *bless* His holy name. Bless the LORD, O my soul, And forget none of His benefits; *Who pardons all your iniquities, Who heals all your diseases; Who redeems your life from the pit, Who crowns you with lovingkindness and compassion; Who satisfies your years with good things,* So that your youth is renewed like the eagle. *The* LORD *performs righteous deeds And judgments for all who are oppressed.* He made known His ways to Moses, His acts to the sons of Israel. *The* LORD *is compassionate and gracious, Slow to anger and abounding in lovingkindness.* He will not always strive *with us,* Nor will He keep *His anger* forever. *He has not dealt with us according to our sins, Nor rewarded us according to our iniquities. For as high as the heavens are above the earth, So great is His lovingkindness toward those who fear Him. As far as the east is from the west, So far has He removed our transgressions from us. Just as a father has compassion on his children, So the* LORD *has compassion on those who fear Him* (emphasis mine).

There are a lot of precious promises found in those verses as well as a beautiful description of what God is like. It's almost as if the psalmist picked up a paintbrush and painted a portrait with his words. It's as if every attribute, way, and act of God is a unique color used to paint such a masterpiece.

He pardons. He heals. He crowns you with love and compassion. He goes into action for those who are oppressed. He's gracious and compassionate. He's slow to anger and abounding in love. He has not treated us according to our sins; rather, He has completely removed them from us. Truly, the psalmist describes the very thing the angel of the Lord declared to the shepherds who were huddled together in a field watching over their flocks the night Jesus was born. "Do not be afraid; for behold, I bring you *good news of great joy*." (See Luke 2:10.)

The great joy is the result of the good news. And the greatest news of all is a God who forgives, a God who pardons and does not hold our trespasses against us.

And yet everything that the psalmist described concerning God and everything that has been written thus far about His heart for us and His desire to find every person will not profit any single one person unless we mix what we have heard with faith. Hebrews 11:1 tells us that faith is the assurance of things hoped for, the conviction of things not seen. In short, faith is in operation when we are utterly convinced of whatever it is we believe even when feelings and circumstances are contrary. For example:

> *Even when life is falling apart all around me and I seem to be all alone, I am still convinced that God loves me because He sent His son.*
> *Even when the bills are stacking up all around me, I am still convinced that I'm more precious than many sparrows and that all things will be added to me and that He knows what I need before I ask*

We know we are convinced when we are unmoved and unshaken and when all you can see is that He who promised is faithful. (See Hebrews 10:23.)

The profit of faith is the reward of what it is that you were seeking and believing. It's the manifestation of what was unseen to your natural eye but very much alive through the eyes of your heart. The profit of faith in everything that's been described up to this point concerning who God is and what He's done is the transformation of life. You know who you are. He's changed your heart. Everything you used to love concerning sin, you now hate. Everything you used to resist and hate concerning God, you now love. It's called being born-again. It's called receiving a new father and seeing life through a clear eye that was once darkened so your whole body will be full of light. (See Matthew 6:22.)

The only way I know how to mix, unite, release faith in what it is that I have heard is to continue hearing it! Romans 10:17 says that faith *comes* from hearing, and hearing by the word of Christ. One of the ways that I hear is I take what it is that I have discovered or read in the word and I pray it out between God and me. In other words, I meditate on what it is I am seeing in the word (which I will discuss in greater detail in a later chapter), because sometimes you hear with your eyes. For example, let's say that I stumbled across John 3:16. "For God so loved the world, that He gave His only begotten Son, that whoever believes in Him shall not perish, but have eternal life."

This is what my prayer would sound like: "Father, I thank you that you love me. You love me because you gave Your Son. Thank you for loving me enough to come and find me and to save me. Thank you that all I have to do is believe in Jesus. You fulfilled what I could not. You did what I could not do in the weakness of my flesh. You sent Jesus to die on my behalf so that I might live and all I have to do is receive that. Thanks for making me brand-new. Thanks for saving my life and for causing me to live."

Truthfully, I could keep praying. I'm convinced that what was just modeled is what fellowship with God looks like. You affirm in your heart what you know to be true and you grow up into it. By doing so, you're allowing the very word you are reading to become flesh within you. You're releasing faith into what it is that you are reading and you are praying with thanksgiving. You can honestly take one verse like John 3:16 and pray that one verse until it gets so large in your heart it's all you can see.

Like I mentioned earlier in this book, "*It's time to see. It's time to believe.*"

We have been forgiven. We are loved. He really came to seek and to save that which was lost. Do we really *believe* that? Are we fully convinced and fully persuaded? Are we still falling apart when someone doesn't return our phone call? Are we shaken when what we are walking through doesn't seem to line up with what we read about in the scriptures? Have we been reduced to thinking we believe something only to find out that when it's put to the test we try to take matters into our own hands? Have we forgotten why trials exist? Are we seeing with our eyes and thinking with our minds rather than hearing with our ears and believing with our heart? Are we a different breed of people on the earth or do we respond to hardship in the same manner as the person who has no profession of faith in Christ? Do we see adversity as an opportunity to shine or as an opportunity to whine?

What would it really look like to truly believe in what we say we believe? God forbid we've been taught we believe something that we are incapable of manifesting. God forbid we've sat in church our whole life believing we believe in the love of God only to continuously be looking for it in all the wrong places. God forbid we've been taught that we are forgiven to only wake up every morning feeling disqualified by what we thought about or did yesterday.

Faith *looks* like something. Faith is more than a confession of words. It's your life taking on what you believe. You become clothed in it. Faith is something you wear, not something you talk about. True faith in what God has spoken through His Son will always result in the word becoming flesh in your life. You become joined to it. In the same way that you can't separate God from His word because He is His word (John 1:1); faith causes you and God's word to become one. As a result, the life you live becomes your words. Your life testifies of what you believe. You don't have to discuss it, argue about it, or try to convince someone that you have it. You simply live it.

The Nature of the Kingdoms

Faith is one of the, if not *the* most powerful, substances on the planet. As we read about earlier, faith is conviction. It's assurance.

And for most of my life, I had released faith into the wrong realities. One of the things that we must understand is that Satan is an opportunist. He will wait for opportune times in your life to whisper lies to you. He did it with Jesus. "When the devil had finished every temptation, he left Him until an *opportune time*" (Luke 4:13).

It's also imperative that we understand how the kingdoms work (the kingdom of God and the kingdom of darkness). The kingdoms are established and grown through the sowing of seed:

> Jesus presented another parable to them, saying, "The kingdom of heaven may be compared to a man who sowed good seed in his field. But while his men were sleeping, his enemy came and sowed tares among the wheat, and went away."
>
> Matthew 13:24–25

Both kingdoms work through the sewing of seed because each kingdom seeks to reproduce itself after its own kind. In Genesis 3:15, God declares to the serpent that He will place enmity between the serpent's seed and Eve's seed. The seed of Eve is Christ Jesus. First Peter 1:23 tells us that we are born again by the imperishable seed—the living and enduring word of God! The implication is whichever seed you are born of reveals who your father is.

The seed that is sown is the word of each kingdom. In God's kingdom truth is sown. In the kingdom of darkness lies are sown. Because Adam and Eve heeded the word of the serpent, they were born of his seed. As a result, we were all born into the transgression of Adam, which is why we needed to be born again.

Whichever seed (or voice) you give credence or your yes to will become the eye you see life through. That does not mean that because you may have believed a lie after you were born again that you suddenly became born of the enemy as if you lost your salvation. Rather, Satan seeks to father all people though his lies. He seeks to deceive the nations.

The kingdoms are empowered through agreement, through faith. Satan's whole goal, in fact, is to get you to agree with what he is saying in order to keep you from what *has been said*. Remember that in these last days, God *has spoken* to us through His Son (Heb. 1:2). Like I had mentioned in the introduction, Satan wants nothing more than to blind your mind in order to keep you from the light of the gospel that's seen through the glory of Christ. (See 2 Corinthians 4:4.) He doesn't do this by blindfolding you or by blinding you naturally. He accomplishes his task by getting you to *see* something other than the truth.

Where we set our eyes and what we give our ears to is very important. The greatest example of what I'm referring to is found in the place we've already been exploring—Genesis 3. The enemy slithers into the garden and begins to bring into question all that God had spoken to Eve concerning the image and likeness she was created in. After a few exchanges of dialogue, Eve begins to release faith into what Satan is saying and now begins to *see* with desire in her eyes the very tree that she and Adam were forbidden to eat from. This is how he blinds the mind of the unbelieving. He wants you to see and taste of the reality he is portraying, but God wants you to taste and see His (Ps. 34:8).

A more practical example can be taken from my own life. I was rejected a lot as a child. It was a spiritual strategy of the enemy to rob me of my identity and fill me with hurt and pain so that when I heard the good news of the gospel, it wouldn't even sound like good news. Because of the amount of failed relationships and abandonment in my life, I began to believe that I wasn't good enough, that I'd always be alone, and that I'm worthy to be rejected. Every relationship that went up in smoke was an opportune time for the enemy to whisper lies to me and his lies always made sense. It made logical, rational, and psychological sense that I would believe those things based on how I was being treated, and as a result, I measured myself that way. But the way others treated me and the things I believed as a result wasn't the truth about me. Christ is the truth about my life. How He has treated me and what He says about me is what's true. The people who hurt me simply didn't know the love of God. Had they known it, they never would have done the things they did. If you can't love your neighbor as you love yourself (see Matthew 22:39), then you can't give or be to others what you don't have for you. If someone is incapable of loving someone else, it's because they don't love themselves. More than that, you can't even love yourself unless you let God love you first. (See 1 John 4:19.)

The gist is that we need to start releasing faith in the right things, not the wrong things. It's time to disempower the lie by agreeing with the truth. Jesus said that if we continue in His word, then we are truly His disciples. Not only that, but we will know the truth and the truth will make us free. (See John 8:31–32.) I tell people this all the time: the two most important words in those verses are *if you*. *You* have to continue in His word. Stop continuing in the lies you've been fed your whole life about what the answer is and what it looks like. Stop continuing in the word of your experience. Stop being a disciple of your past. The enemy has worked so hard to keep you from the truth that you will read about later on. He doesn't want you to see the light of this gospel because if the light comes on within you, the darkness has nowhere to hide. Let's see this thing for what it really is. Let's see the simplicity and the beauty of a God who came to find His children and not only that but loves and forgives them.

What's Next?

Everything I was ever looking for in life is found in Him. There are probably no greater stories in the Bible that encapsulate this reality more than the ones found in Luke 7:36–50, John 4:5–26, and John 8:2–11. In fact, it's because of these women's stories found within these verses that has caused me to write this book. They embody humanity's search for God and His search for humanity. They are the reflection of a person who experiences great joy over what it is that they have found. For the first time in their lives, they found the very thing they have been searching for, and they come alive! Their lives testify of what it looks like to believe that God loves you and forgives you. These women model what it looks like to be lost and to be found.

"For the Son of Man has come to seek and to save that which was lost" (Luke 19:10).

Tears, Perfume, and Feet

How lovely on the mountains are the feet of him who brings good news, Who announces peace And brings good news of happiness, Who announces salvation, *And* says to Zion, "Your God reigns!"

—Isaiah 52:7

"How beautiful are the feet of those who bring good news of good things!" (Rom. 10:15).

Alabaster Box
by Cece Winans[1]

The room grew still as she made her way to Jesus
She stumbles through the tears that made her blind
She felt such pain
Some spoke in anger
Heard folks whisper, "There's no place here for her kind"
Still on she came through the shame that flushed her face
Until at last, she knelt before his feet
And though she spoke no words,
everything she said was heard

As she poured her love for the Master
from her box of alabaster

And I've come to pour my praise on Him
like oil from Mary's alabaster box
Don't be angry if I wash his feet with my
tears and I dry them with my hair
You weren't there the night He found me
You did not feel what I felt when He
wrapped his love all around me and
You don't know the cost of the oil in my alabaster box

I can't forget the way life used to be
I was a prisoner to the sin that had me bound
And I spent my days
Poured my life without measure into a little
treasure box I'd thought I'd found
Until the day when Jesus came to me and healed
my soul with the wonder of His touch
So now I'm giving back to Him all
the praise He's worthy of
I've been forgiven and that's why I love Him so much

And I've come to pour my praise on Him
like oil from Mary's alabaster box
Don't be angry if I wash his feet with my
tears and dry them with my hair
You weren't there the night Jesus found me
You did not feel what I felt when He wrapped
his loving arms around me and
You don't know the cost of the oil
Oh, you don't know the cost of my praise
You don't know the cost of the oil
In my alabaster box

We Should Probably Start Here

The woman with the alabaster vial of perfume found in Luke's gospel has become one of my favorite stories in the Bible. The truth be told, all of my favorite stories in the gospels center around Jesus's one-on-one encounter with women (the woman at the well, the woman caught in adultery, and the woman with the alabaster vial of perfume). Although I haven't fully researched this to be completely true, it seems to me that no person's sin is talked about or placed out in the open for all to see like the women Jesus comes face to face with in the gospels. Even though they appear exposed and naked through their trespasses, it only causes their interaction with Jesus to be all the more beautiful. They had finally found who and what they had been seeking for their whole lives. Where sin increased, grace abounded all the more. (See Romans 5:20.) The ugliness of their past met the beauty of their future found through His love and forgiveness.

To me, their stories are the climax of *the story*. They embody the heartbeat of the gospel. In fact, in three of the four Gospels—Matthew, Mark, and John—we read this account concerning the woman with the alabaster vial.

> Now when Jesus was in Bethany, at the home of Simon the leper, a woman came to Him with an alabaster vial of very costly perfume, and she poured it on His head as He reclined *at the table*. But the disciples were indignant when they saw *this*, and said, "Why this waste? For this *perfume* might have been sold for a high price and *the money* given to the poor." But Jesus, aware of this, said to them, "Why do you bother the woman? For she has done a good deed to Me. For you always have the poor with you; but you do not always have Me. For when she poured this perfume on My body, she did it to prepare Me for burial. *Truly I say to you, wherever this gospel is preached in the whole world, what*

this woman has done will also be spoken of in memory of her"
(emphasis mine).

Matthew 26:6–13

Whenever I read that last verse, I'm always amazed by the fact that two thousand years later, we are still discussing what this woman did! Jesus was right! If what this woman did will be spoken of whenever the Gospel is preached, we probably ought to start with her story.

It's important to note here that many scholars are unsure as to whether or not the person described in these verses is the same person described in Luke 7:36–50 (whom we will take a look at in a moment). Many scholars say it's *not* the same person based on the time frame in which these stories take place. The accounts found in Matthew 26:6–13, Mark 14:3–9, and John 12:1–8 date the woman pouring her perfume upon Jesus just moments before His arrest and crucifixion. The account found in Luke 7 takes place well before Jesus's arrest and crucifixion. As a result, many people see these stories as separate from one another and not the same.

John's gospel is the only gospel to point out that the woman's name attached to this act of preparing Jesus for burial just before His arrest and crucifixion is Mary. (See John 12:3.) It's the same Mary who is both sister to Martha and Lazarus. In fact, John's gospel also makes this statement concerning Mary. It was the Mary who *anointed* the Lord with ointment, and wiped His feet with her hair, whose brother Lazarus was sick" (John 11:2; emphasis mine).

Why is this verse important? It's important because what's described above is recorded before Mary does what she does in John 12:3 where she takes perfume of pure nard and anoints Jesus' feet with it while wiping His feet with her hair. Why make mention of an act that hadn't happened yet unless John is referring to an act that *did* already happen? He said it was the Mary who *anointed* not *will anoint*. What if John is referring to what's recorded in Luke 7:36–50? He certainly would have been there.

Because the identity of the woman found in Luke 7 is up for debate, I am not completely sold on the fact that it's *not* the same woman found at the end of the other gospels performing what seems to be a repeat of what had been done in Luke 7. It seems probable to me that if you've already done something of great significance, you are more likely to do it again because of the meaning attached to it. I believe that the woman found at the feet of Jesus in Luke 7 is the same person found in the other accounts. I believe the identity of this person is none other than Mary herself, the same Mary who is found sitting at Jesus's feet, hanging on His every word, choosing the good part. (See Luke 10:38–42.) Indeed, it seems as though she hasn't left the posture she first approached Him through—being at His feet! It seems way too improbable to me to have two separate women committing the same act. I believe Mary was repeating the same act yet with two separate motivations. I'll explain the difference.

In the account that we read about above in Matthew 26, we see that the woman poured the very costly perfume on Jesus's body to prepare Him for burial. Why? Is it really that hard to understand why the disciples responded the way they did? Isn't their argument *rational* and *logical?* Couldn't they have used the costly contents within the alabaster vial to care for many people? Wouldn't that have been the right thing to do? Isn't that what Jesus would have done? After all, it's a godly principle to care for the poor.

Come on. Think with me.

Put yourself in the shoes of the disciples. They have seen countless people down and out along the stretch of their three year journey with Jesus. They've seen beggars of alms. They've seen the broken and downtrodden. They watched the Master heal the blind eyes of the poor. They heard the words of Jesus to the rich young ruler instructing him to sell his possessions and give to the poor in order that he might be complete and have treasure in heaven. (See Matthew 19:21.) They saw bread and fish multiplied through their hands to feed the many thousands. Wouldn't it have been right to sell the perfume at a high price and give the money to those in need? Not in heaven's eyes.

The truth is that this woman caught a revelation that the disciples were unable to see in the three years they had been following Him. I believe it was a revelation built upon the first act she committed with the alabaster vial in Luke 7, the very story we will soon look at. What she did for Jesus was the very thing He was getting ready to do for her. That alabaster vial of perfume was what Matthew's gospel describes above as *costly*. There was a price tag associated with it. It was expensive. And yet its cost was nothing to be compared with the price that Jesus was about to pay

"For when she poured this perfume on My body, she did it to prepare Me for burial" (Matt. 26:12).

Jesus was about to die, or better yet, Jesus was about to spend it all.

"For you have been bought with a price" (1 Cor. 6:20).

And this woman with her alabaster vial of expensive perfume understood this. She saw the price He was about to pay and she was willing to shower Him with the price of her affection. That vial represented everything she had found in Him since the first vial she poured out in Luke 7. It's interesting that the first time she pours out her perfume she pours it upon Jesus's feet (Luke 7:38) and then on His head the second time (Matt. 26:7). Why? At His feet she found everything she was looking for and upon His head she pours out all that she's found.

Romans 12:1 urges us by the mercies of God to present our bodies as a living and holy sacrifice. Such an act is acceptable to God and it is our spiritual service of worship. Is this not what Jesus did? Did He not lay down His life for us and was He not raised from the dead by the Spirit of holiness? (See Romans 1:4.) Although the laying down of His life was a holy sacrifice, He was made alive through resurrection. His life truly was a *living* and *holy* sacrifice. He came alive through death, and it's no different for us. To die is to live. We were never created for ourselves. We were created for His image and likeness.

Jesus spent it all and the Father highly exalted Him and bestowed on Him the name that is above every name. (See Philippians 2:9.) His life and death were the contents within His alabaster vial poured out freely for us. I believe Mary understood this and that her act of pouring her perfume on His body was her way of saying, "In the same way you are about to do it for me, I'm going to do it for You. From this day forward, I will live my life in the same way as You did as a living and holy sacrifice." Her act was her Romans 12:1 moment. Her extravagance was a life laid down, the ultimate service of worship.

The Damsel not in Distress

Without further adieu, let's jump into the book and chapter of the story that truthfully became the catalyst in writing this book in the first place. Truly, we must understand what she found and understood.

> Now one of the Pharisees was requesting Him to dine with him, and He entered the Pharisee's house and reclined *at the table.* And there was a woman in the city who was a sinner; and when she learned that He was reclining *at the table* in the Pharisee's house, she brought an alabaster vial of perfume, and standing behind *Him* at His feet, weeping, she began to wet His feet with her tears, and kept wiping them with the hair of her head, and kissing His feet and anointing them with the perfume. Now when the Pharisee who had invited Him saw this, he said to himself, "If this man were a prophet He would know who and what sort of person this woman is who is touching Him, that she is a sinner." And Jesus answered him, "Simon, I have something to say to you." And he replied, "Say it, Teacher." "A moneylender had two debtors: one owed five hundred denarii, and the other fifty. When they were unable to repay, he graciously forgave them both. So which of them will love

him more?" Simon answered and said, "I suppose the one whom he forgave more." And He said to him, "You have judged correctly." Turning toward the woman, He said to Simon, "Do you see this woman? I entered your house; you gave Me no water for My feet, but she has wet My feet with her tears and wiped them with her hair. You gave Me no kiss; but she, since the time I came in, has not ceased to kiss My feet. You did not anoint My head with oil, but she anointed My feet with perfume. For this reason I say to you, her sins, which are many, have been forgiven, for she loved much; but he who is forgiven little, loves little." Then He said to her, "Your sins have been forgiven." Those who were reclining *at the table* with Him began to say to themselves, "Who is this *man* who even forgives sins?" And He said to the woman, "Your faith has saved you; go in peace."

Luke 7:36–50

This woman, brave and bold as she was, embodies what it means to once be lost and to now be found. One of the things that I seek to do when reading the scriptures is to not be too quick to *read the scriptures*. Let me explain. The last thing I want to do, personally speaking, is to read the Bible in such a way that it becomes a box with a check mark in it on my list of things to do on any given day. My relationship with God is so much more than a devotional time. I'm not seeking to devote time to Him. I want to become like Him. I don't want to miss anything that He might be trying to speak to me through His word. I don't want to be in a rush. I want to take my time. I want what I'm reading to become who I am. I want to understand. I want to see. I want to believe. In other words, I don't simply want to read the word. I want it to read me.

I say all of that because there is so much within these fifteen verses you just read. There's emotion. There's truth. There's redemption. There's freedom. There's grace. There's beauty. And I don't want to miss an ounce of it.

As we look at this passage of scripture together, the first thing I'd like to draw attention to is the posture of the woman. We read that she is a sinner and that she brought with her an alabaster vial of perfume and that she began to wet Jesus's feet with her tears and wipe His feet with her hair. She also kissed His feet and began to anoint them with the perfume. Because I'm a "word guy," I'd like to show you what the word *wet* actually means through the Greek language this passage was originally written in (word guy: someone who has a deep affection for the word of God and seeks to understand it through meditation and study. That's Brian Connolly's definition and that's for free!) The word *wet* is pronounced this way in the Greek: *brecho* meaning to send rain or to rain. Why is this significant? It's significant because it tells us this woman wasn't simply crying. Her tears weren't just rolling down her cheeks onto His feet. No. This woman would have been sobbing. She would have been undone. And it's reasonable to assume that wailing would have accompanied such sobbing. In short, this woman would have been drawing significant attention to herself not only because she was a woman doing the unthinkable in that culture by approaching a man, let alone a rabbi in such a manner but because of her tears, because of her posture. Indeed, she is the epitome of what it means to approach the throne of grace with confidence. (See Hebrews 4:16.)

The question that needs answered concerning this woman is, What would cause a person to be sending rain upon someone's feet with their tears? What could move someone to that extent to respond in such a way? I believe the answer is found in this statement: when the tears of your past meet the beauty of the feet that bring good news, you're forever changed. What you used to spend on yourself you now spend on Him in the exchange of beauty for ashes. (See Isaiah 61:3.)

Remember, this passage introduces this woman as a sinner. It's not the "nicest" of introductions now, is it? But it *was* her reality. It *was* what she was caught up in. It *was* who she used to be. Such an indictment isn't only true about this particular woman.

It would have been an appropriate description of all of us outside of Christ.

> And *you* were dead in your trespasses and sins, in which *you* formerly walked according to the course of this world, according to the prince of the power of the air, of the spirit that is now working in the sons of disobedience. *Among them we too all formerly lived in the lusts of our flesh, indulging the desires of the flesh and of the mind, and were by nature children of wrath, even as the rest* (emphasis mine).

> Ephesians 2:1–3

In a nutshell, we were all fathered by someone else outside of our relationship with Christ. We all followed the counsel of something else. All of us were like sheep that had gone astray and followed after our own way. (See Isaiah 53:6.) And yet the reality is that we all did what we did in ignorance. We didn't know the truth. We didn't know what to put faith in until Christ came, the image of the invisible God. (See Galatians 3:22–23, Colossians 1:15.) If we had, we never would have done what we did. As a result, God has overlooked the times of ignorance and is declaring to all people through His Son that we should change our minds about who we are, who He is, and what we are doing because there is a day that He has fixed when He will judge the world in righteousness through a Man (Jesus) that He has raised from the dead as proof. (See Acts 17:30–31.) Indeed, God is shouting for all to come home through the sacrifice of His Son and to receive the adoption as His sons and daughters, to be what we were always predestined to be. (See Ephesians 1:5.)

That is exactly what this woman did.

It is my personal conviction that this woman found at Jesus's feet everything she had been looking for her whole life. Why do I believe this? Isaiah 52:7 and Romans 10:15 hold the answer:

"How lovely on the mountains are the feet of him who brings good news, Who announces peace And brings good news of hap-

piness, Who announces salvation, *And* says to Zion, "Your God reigns!" (Isa. 52:7; emphasis mine).

"How beautiful are the feet of those who bring good news of good things!" (Rom. 10:15; emphasis mine).

This woman recognized the news these feet came to declare. Her tears reveal two things—first, her repentance from who she was and how she used to live and second, the joy of what she found.

Her tears were not only the tears that flow from Godly sorrow that produces repentance; they were tears of joy. Her search was over. This story captures the essence of the irony that both parties were looking for one another. She was looking for Jesus. Jesus was looking for her. And when the two search parties meet, heaven goes bananas, and lives are forever changed.

Luke 7:37 says, "When she learned that He was reclining at the table of the Pharisee's house, she brought an alabaster vial of perfume." It doesn't say, "When she learned about Him." She learned of His location and brought with her all that she was. She didn't have the alabaster vial with her. She had to go get it. She programmed her GPS and went to where He was. This tells me that she was looking for Him, and when she discovered where He was, she brought with her all that she was and did up to that moment. She gave Him every mistake, every failure, and every sin. She gave her very life—the thing of greatest cost and she poured it out upon Him.

If we knew where He was, would we spend on Him that which is most meaningful to us? Would we give it all up in appreciation, just for one moment at His feet? Would we cash in what was never ours in the first place?

The price you pay for something is always synonymous with the joy you find through it. It's because of the joy over the treasure the man finds in the field that he goes and sells all he has to purchase it. (See Matthew 13:44.) It's because of the joy over the treasure you and I are to God that heaven spent all that it had only to replenish its bank account with every saved soul. And it's because of the joy over what this woman found that she took all that she used to spend on herself and poured it out upon the feet that came to declare good news to her.

The tears of this woman reveal that the life she once spent on herself has now collided with the kindness of God. She understands she's not forgotten. She's not a throw away. She's home. She's precious to her Father, and He is precious to her. That's why she pours the perfume over Jesus. In Him, she has found everything she's been looking for. She's found love. She's found acceptance. She's found forgiveness. Whereas heaven gave up everything to purchase these realities for this once lost daughter, she is willing to give up everything to obtain what heaven paid for.

It's a paradox, really. The gift that God offers is free and yet it will cost you everything. It's free because it's never about what you have done based on your own merit. It's about what He has done. All you need to do is say yes to it and receive it. The cost, however, is your life. The cost is everything you accumulated through the fall of man and everything life taught you that the cross doesn't declare. The cost is you dethroning yourself as God and allowing Him to take His rightful place in your life because all things were made by Him, for Him, and through Him. (See John 1:3 and Colossians 1:16.) It's leaving the nature of selfishness and putting on the nature of love.

Whereas we often see this woman's pouring out of her perfume upon Jesus's feet as an act of worship, I see it as something much bigger. Don't get me wrong. I'm not saying it's not an act of worship. I just believe there is something far greater and deeper going on and it's worth examining it. I believe the contents of her alabaster vial is everything she was and everything she spent on herself before this very moment. I believe it's the ashes of her past and that it represents everything she was living for before this moment. I believe it represents the very thing the younger brother did in Luke 15. He took his inheritance and spent it upon himself. Likewise, I believe she took her inheritance called life and spent it on herself. Her very act stands in direct opposition to what the man did in the parable that Jesus told in Luke 12:16–21.

In this parable, Jesus tells the story about a man whose land was very productive. Because he did not have enough space to store all that his land was producing, he tore down his existing storage structures and built bigger ones. After the completion of his construction and storage of his goods, the man decided that his soul could finally rest and that he could eat, drink, and be merry. He was ready to party. God then rains on this man's parade by saying, "You fool! This very night your soul is required of you, and now, who will own what you have prepared?" Jesus then ends the parable with this statement: "So is the man who stores up treasure for himself, and is not rich toward God" (Luke 12:21).

What is this type of man like? *A fool.* (That's some pretty strong language!)

That alabaster vial was the treasure the woman stored up for herself but it was nothing compared to the treasure that she found in Him. And that's the key, isn't it? Until Jesus becomes personal, until we meet Him, we won't pour out what we've accumulated for ourselves upon Him. It's pretty radical to think that while we were lost and spending our inheritance on ourselves, heaven spent all that it had on us. Heaven gave up its most valuable resource to purchase what on the surface looked unbecoming, but was precious through the eyes of God. Why? Heaven always sees a greater reality. Heaven has the capacity to see beyond the surface and to gaze with the eyes of understanding.

The Dragonfly

I pay attention to things. I especially pay attention to things that seemingly reoccur over and over again. I pay attention to things I see. I pay attention to things I hear. And I pay attention to what's going on around me. I'm always looking for the deeper meaning of things. I'm always seeking to understand the *why* behind the *what*. I'm not sure if all of my years as an English major at

Millersville University shaped this habit within me while reading many types of literature in the pursuit of identifying the symbolism within what I was reading or if it's the way God wired me. Either way, I'm always looking beyond the surface.

In the summer of 2012, I began to notice that I was seeing a certain flying friend, a dragonfly, almost everywhere I went. I would see him sitting at a traffic light of a busy intersection. I would see him outside of my house. I would see him in places where there was absolutely no body of water to be found within close proximity. But the strangest place of all that I took notice of my buddy was in a graveyard called Mt. Rose Cemetery. As weird and as creepy as this might sound, I would often drive into the graveyard, park my car at its highest point, get out, and pray. It was peaceful, and it overlooked a vast portion of the surrounding area where my church, Praise Community, is found. Once I saw a dragonfly occupying and hovering around my place of prayer, I said to myself, "That's it. Why do I keep seeing you guys?" Desperate for an answer, I pulled out my smartphone and searched for the meaning of dragonflies on Google. Whereas some people might have cautioned me to not use such a resource in search for a spiritual answer, I believe God spoke exactly what He needed to speak to me through the very first website that popped up in the search engine.

Although there is much to say concerning what it is that I found on the website, let me point out this particular snippet of information because I believe it will be helpful in understanding what it is that God is doing today and will help to further drive home the point of what is happening between Jesus and this woman with the alabaster vial of perfume:

The traditional association of dragonflies with water also gives rise to this meaning to this amazing insect. The dragonfly's scurrying flight across the water represents an act of going beyond what's on the surface and looking deeper into the implications and aspects of life.[2]

These two sentences on that website carried incredible significance for me on that day when I read them. I read those words in the midst of a fast and in the midst of crying out to God to just simply love people and to see them the way He does. I got to a place that summer where I said to God, "If I can't love people the way you do, just pull the plug on me now. Take me out of ministry. I don't want to do this without seeing what you see."

I prayed that way because I wanted what I read in 2 Corinthians 5:14–16 to be my reality.

> For the love of Christ controls us, having concluded this, *that one died for all, therefore all died*; and He died for all, so that they who live might no longer live for themselves, but for Him who died and rose again on their behalf. Therefore *from now on we recognize no one according to the flesh*; even though we have known Christ according to the flesh, yet now we know *Him in this way* no longer.

I've loved 2 Corinthians 5:14 for as long as I can remember. I want what Paul is writing about to become my motivation for all things. I want to be controlled by the love of Christ and the only way to do that is to fellowship long enough with the phrase that immediately follows Paul's declaration, "Having concluded this, that one died for all." Indeed, in those words of Paul lies the secret to how the love of Christ controlled him. He concluded that one died for all. The barometer of God's love for humanity is Christ crucified for every human being. Paul understood this and he fellowshipped with it. As a result, Paul didn't see people according to the flesh. He didn't judge them at face value. They weren't books to be weighed by their cover. They were so much more than that. They were people whom Christ died for. They were people that were worth the blood of Christ. Paul didn't esteem them for their mistakes. He saw their value.

This is exactly what Jesus did with the woman at His feet.

It's pretty staggering and humbling to think that the feet that rest upon a footstool called earth (see Isaiah 66:1) and will one day also rest upon a footstool made up of His enemies (see Hebrews 10:13) allowed the tears of a sinner to stain them.

That's amazing grace.

I believe God wants us to see beyond the surface. In fact, I believe He is opening our eyes to see the value of human life and the price He paid for everyone to come alive within us. I believe a day is coming and now is where we will not judge a book by its cover but by its value. The value of a thing, after all, is determined by the price one pays for it.

Seeing Through Heaven's Eyes

Remember, in Luke 7:37, we read that the woman with the alabaster vial is introduced to us readers as a sinner. In Luke 7:39, we read about how Simon, the Pharisee who invited Jesus to dine with him, truly sees and feels about this woman. It says, "Now when the Pharisee who had invited Him saw this, he said to himself, 'If this man were a prophet He would know who and what sort of person this woman is who is touching Him, that she is a sinner'" (Luke 7:39).

The funny thing is that Jesus knows exactly who she is and what it is that she's caught up in! He's Jesus! In Luke 7:47, Jesus makes mention that her sins are many. He's fully aware of her plight. He always knows why we do what we do. He knows what people are looking for and He knows that if they truly found it, they wouldn't be doing what they're doing. If people truly understood the value and integrity and honor of their lives, they would never act as the fool who returns to his folly or like a dog that returns to its vomit. (See Proverbs 26:11.) Jesus is so much bigger than our mistakes and our perilous searches for who we are. If Jesus measured us according to what we've done rather than who we always were in His heart, we'd all be toast! He wouldn't have come to find and save us. He would have come to punish us. He wouldn't have come with "good news." He would have come with certificates of divorce.

Even though Jesus had the knowledge about what sort of person this woman was, He was not shocked nor taken aback by what it was that she had done (her sins were many). Rather, He restored her dignity by saying to Simon, "Do you *see* this woman?" (See Luke 7:44.) Simon saw a sinner. Jesus saw a woman, a daughter worth forgiving, and He was inviting Simon to *see* what He saw.

Indeed, Jesus was also inviting Simon to see what it was that this woman saw as well. Jesus was impressed and moved by her faith. How do I know this to be true? Take a look at Luke 7:50, "And He said to the woman, '*Your faith* has saved you; go in peace'" (emphasis mine).

What You See, You Declare

Let's review. What's faith again? The *assurance* of things hoped for, the *conviction* of things not seen. This woman saw the assurance of everything she had ever been hoping for. She finally found everything she had ever been searching for. She had the conviction that she was forgiven before Jesus's pronouncement over her in the above verse. I know this because of what we read in Luke 7:47. "For this reason I say to you, her sins, which are many, have been forgiven, for she loved much; but he who is forgiven little, loves little."

The last time I checked, the number 47 comes before the number 50. In verse 47, Jesus makes mention that her sins are forgiven, but in verse 50 He reveals why "*your faith has saved you.*" She *saw her forgiveness* and *believed it* before He spoke it. I believe that she saw at His feet the very thing He was willing to do for her feet. (See John 13:3–5.) I believe she saw a god who had come to wash her feet and didn't demand that she'd wash His. It's because of what she saw and knew to be true about Jesus that she did what she did. All the heartache, all the letdown, all of the stops along the journey of life where she tried to find herself was answered and found in the house of Simon the Pharisee.

Although the scripture does not indicate what sins she had committed or what sort of person this woman was, I'd like to speculate here a little bit. If you'll allow me, I'd like to take a little liberty here based on the other two women I'll be writing about in the upcoming chapters. As I said earlier, to my knowledge no one else's sin is exploited or put on display in the gospels as much as these three women, which makes their story of redemption all the more powerful. The other two women I'll be writing about were found in the arms of men. What if—and again, I'm only speculating—the woman with the alabaster vial was no different? What if she was the sort of person who gave herself to the oldest profession in the world? What if she was a woman of ill repute? What if she thought the answer to her significance and value was found in the affirmation of men? What if the source of her tears was the evidence of her joy that she had finally found *the man*, Christ Jesus, the Lord?

Whatever her sins were and whatever sort of person she was before Christ, she saw herself as forgiven. As a result, she loved Him through what she poured out upon Him. Her tears and her posture declared what she believed. Her faith had saved her! The truth is that we will always live out what we understand. Our lives declare what we see and what we believe. Paul understood this better than anyone else. Galatians 2:20 revealed how he lived. "I have been crucified with Christ; and it is no longer I who live, but Christ lives in me; and the *life* which I now live in the flesh I live by faith in the Son of God, who loved me and gave Himself up for me."

Indeed, Paul saw himself according to what he described and he lived it. He lived it because of what he released faith in—the love and sacrifice of Jesus Christ. This is how I want to live all of my days. I don't simply want to quote this verse. I want to *be* this verse.

It's my belief that if we, like this woman, saw ourselves as forgiven, we'd live forgiven! I believe that if we truly understood the forgiveness of sin, sin would lose its influence in our lives. Isn't that just simple? The reason that certain people love much is because they understand that they've been forgiven much. But before anyone sells themselves short and says that because they weren't a drug addict or a prostitute or any other notorious sinner and therefore can't understand what it means to be forgiven much, let me point out that all of us had sinned and fallen short of the glory of God. (See Romans 3:23.) We were all in the same boat, heading down the same stream. We have all been forgiven, period. Some of us may have manifested worse than others, but we were all children of wrath just the same. (See Ephesians 3:3.) I guess what I'm trying to say is we have all been forgiven much. We just need to understand that.

This woman believed she was forgiven. The evidence for her faith was witnessed through the act of love she poured upon Him. In the same way, the love we have for Jesus is dependent upon our understanding His love for us through His forgiveness. The more we understand our forgiveness, the more we love. The more we love, the more we give because that's what love does. For God so loved the world that He gave. (See John 3:16.)

We must let our faith take us to what this woman found because it is our reality whether we see it or not. We are what He says we are. It's time to get on page with it and live accordingly.

As I mentioned earlier, there are still two other women that we need to read about. Their stories are so precious and so beautiful, and they are my favorites among all the stories in the gospels. The woman with the alabaster vial lived for everything that was in that vial. Similarly, there was another woman that lived for the contents that filled another container. The difference is that this container wasn't a vial, or was the contents perfume. No. The container for this particular woman was a well and the contents were water, but then again, this story isn't simply about H_2O.

H$_2$O

Now on the last day, the great *day* of the feast, Jesus stood and cried out, saying, "If anyone is thirsty, let him come to Me and drink."

—John 7:37

"Blessed are those who hunger and thirst for righteousness, for they shall be satisfied" (Matt. 5:6).

Sweep Me Away
by Nic and Rachael Billman[1]

Sometimes the words are not enough
to say exactly how I feel
Sometimes my songs cannot express
the desire that I have for You
But You hear the groanings
You hear the cries inside my heart
You know the longings
You know the desires hidden inside

So take my hand
Draw me into the truth
Sweep me away to a secret place
Just You and me
Face to face

You hear the groanings
You hear the cries inside my heart
You know the longings
You know the desires hidden inside

I love you
I love you
I love you, My child

Groanings Too Deep For Words

The other morning while I was praying, I heard a voice rise up in my heart. This is what it said: "I'm tired of drinking from other wells." This voice is the byproduct of a deeper groaning that has been taking place within me for quite some time. It's a groaning that I'm all too familiar with. It's the desire to know and experience God in a greater way. It's the roar for more!

In Romans 8, we read about these groanings. Romans 8:19–22 talks about the groanings of creation and its longing for the sons of God to be revealed so that it might be set free from its slavery to corruption. Romans 8:23 highlights the groaning within every born-again believer, namely that we all eagerly await to be clothed with the eternity we've been born into, the redemption of our body and our adoption as sons. And Romans 8:26 reveals, "In the same way the Spirit also helps our weakness; for we do not know how to pray as we should, but the Spirit Himself intercedes for *us with groanings too deep for words*" (emphasis mine).

The truth is that the groanings within you will always be greater than any eloquence of speech you can conjure up through prayer. Your groanings speak louder than words. They are the product of a deep heart cry and they are the result of the Spirit Himself. In my opinion, the very things I groan for within myself are the product of my willingness to get on board with what it is that God wants to accomplish in and through my life. It's the agreement I have with the Spirit of God Himself.

Indeed, I believe that as we delight ourselves in the Lord, He gives us the desires of our heart. (See Psalm 37:4.) The desire that you have within you is the result of your fellowship with God. The things I groan for within myself are not my ideas. They are His. It just so happens that my heart is in agreement with His. I want to become like Him in every way. I want to be used by Him. I want to know Him. I want to cry tears for the lost. I want to love the way He loves. And yet, none of those things are the product of my great thinking. They are the very things He wants for me.

In fact, before we get down to the true nitty-gritty of this chapter, let's take a look at some concrete examples of this principle in action.

Hannah and Shiloh

My wife and I are very strategic when it comes to naming our children. It's our conviction that names carry great meaning and destiny within them, which is why we are all too eager for wanting and expecting God to name our kiddos. As I had mentioned in a previous chapter, my wife and I were taken aback in February of 2013 when we had received the knowledge that we were pregnant with identical twin girls. Interestingly enough, my wife and I knew instantly within our hearts that one of our girls was going to be named Hannah, but we just couldn't agree on the name of the other twin. We scratched our heads, threw names out from time to time, but nothing stuck. The names we offered were simply "good ideas" and "what about this name" scenarios.

Finally, one day, my wife says, "What do you think about the name *Shiloh*?" It was as if a bell went off in my brain. *Ding, Ding, Ding, Ding, Ding!* This was the name! "I love it!" I said. I thought we nailed it and that we were in agreement until my wife brought up the following point in conversation. "You know," she said,

"Brad Pitt and Angelina Jolie have a child named Shiloh. Maybe we shouldn't use it."

Do you know how you're supposed to think before you speak? Well, let's just say that didn't happen. My mouth totally bypassed that suggestion and said, "Are you serious! Who cares! I didn't even know that Brad Pitt and Angelina Jolie had a child named Shiloh! We can still use the name."

It wasn't just because Brad Pitt and Angelina Jolie had used the name. Many other reasons as to *why* we shouldn't use Shiloh became more evident and raised a lot of doubt within my wife. She became aware that some people have used the name for boys and dogs. She felt conflicted when family would say things such as "Why would you use a contemporary name like Shiloh when you've used more traditional names for your other girls?"

Don't you love family? They always have an opinion right when you want to hear it the most!

What you are about to read was what I thought was going to be the game changer for my wife. I thought this next event would have completely solidified the use of the name Shiloh, but I was mistaken. I honestly didn't know what it was going to take for this unnamed twin to inherit a name. What happened was my wife had decided to invite her mother to one of the ultrasound appointments for the twins. My mother-in-law had never been to an ultrasound appointment for our two oldest girls, so I thought it was a very sweet and awesome gesture on my wife's part. While at the appointment, the ultrasound tech explained to my mother-in-law that they identified the unborn babies as A and B (great names, huh?). Baby A has always had a reputation of not showing her face during these appointments, and now, my mother-in-law was witnessing this for herself.

Would you like to know what she said about this? Check this out. My mother-in-law says, "Wow. Baby A is really shy. You should name her something with the word *shy* in it."

I'm going to let that sink in for a moment before we go any further.

Silence.

Aah! Are you serious? *Come on, Nicole!* was what I was thinking when Nicole recounted to me what her mother said. If that's not God, I don't know what is! I finally said to her, "Come on, babe. I think God is really trying to get our attention. Your mom had no idea that we were even thinking of using the name Shiloh."

Honestly, guys, the evidence was still not convincing enough for my wife! This certainly doesn't make her a bad person. She needed something more definitive. She wasn't interested in coincidences. She wanted to hear directly from God for herself. Truthfully, I'm glad she had that kind of hunger and here's why. In July of 2013, the Lord wanted me to read about Hannah in the Bible. I turned to 1 Samuel 1 not fully knowing what to expect, but after reading a few verses, everything became freakishly crystal clear! Here's what I read:

> Now there was a certain man from Ramathaim-zophim from the hill country of Ephraim, and his name was Elkanah the son of Jeroham, the son of Elihu, the son of Tohu, the son of Zuph, an Ephraimite. He had two wives: the name of one was Hannah and the name of the other Peninnah; and Peninnah had children, but Hannah had no children. Now this man would go up from his city yearly to worship and to sacrifice to the LORD of hosts in *Shiloh*. And the two sons of Eli, Hophni and Phinehas, were priests to the LORD there (emphasis mine).
>
> 1 Samuel 1:1–3

Are you freaking out right now? You should be! I know I did, and I immediately texted all of 1 Samuel 1 to my wife and awaited her reply. It was what she needed. It was the confirmation she was looking for. And now we have two beautiful and healthy baby girls named Hannah and Shiloh (sorry, Brad and Angelina).

Relentless and Desperate

I love the story of Hannah. She was married to a man by the name of Elkanah, and he was married to another woman by the name of Peninnah. Peninnah is what we English majors would call the "antagonist" in this story. Year after year, Elkanah would venture up to Shiloh (where Joshua had pitched the tent of meeting) to sacrifice to and worship the Lord. When the day came for Elkanah to sacrifice, he would give portions to Peninnah and her children, but he would give Hannah a double portion because of his love for her. Even though the Lord had closed up her womb, Elkanah had a deep seeded affection for Hannah.

Peninnah, however, would provoke Hannah to bitterness and irritation when she would lord over Hannah the fact that she had many children and Hannah had none. Hannah's rival would often drive her to tears and loss of appetite. While Elkanah witnessed the tears of his bride fall from her face, he'd ask, "Hannah, why do you weep and why do you not eat and why is your heart sad? Am I not better to you than ten sons?" (1 Sam. 1:8). The truth is that there was nothing that Elkanah could adorn Hannah with that would satisfy the deep groaning within her. There was no amount of kind and encouraging words that Elkanah could say. There was no amount of fine clothing and fine dining that would raise the countenance of Hannah's face. There was no double portion large enough to fill the void that faced Hannah every time she stared into the eyes of her opponent's children. She wanted a son and the only one who could open her womb was God. He was the only one who could satisfy the longing of her heart, the groaning too deep for words.

One day while praying at the temple, Hannah wept before the Lord as she cried out to Him. Like the woman with the alabaster vial, these were no ordinary tears. These were tears of desperation. Hannah bewailed before God and she made a vow that if the Lord were to remember her and give her a son, she would give him to God all the days of his life.

While Hannah was praying, the priest, Eli, took notice of her. He paid close attention to the fact that her mouth was moving but no sound was being uttered. In a nutshell, Eli surveyed Hannah's mannerisms and concluded that she was drunk and told her to get rid of whatever wine he suspected she was drinking! The truth is that when you pursue God in hunger and desire to live by faith, you will look crazy at times to the world around you. What often justifies you before God (faith) will often condemn you before men. They won't understand. It's foolishness to the unbeliever but its wisdom to God.

After Hannah explains to Eli that she's not drunk but has rather poured out her heart before the Lord concerning her desire for a son, Eli says, "Go in peace; and may the God of Israel grant your petition that you have asked of Him" (1 Sam. 1:17). Hannah then rises from that place, eats, and walks away with her face no longer sad. She had relations with Elkanah the very next day and the Lord remembered her (went into action on her behalf), and she conceived and gave birth to a son, Samuel.

Hannah is the picture of what it looks like to have a groaning within that only God can satisfy because God had placed it there. The truth is that Samuel was not Hannah's idea. He was God's. The word of the Lord was rare in the days that Samuel was born (1 Sam. 3:1), and it was God's plan to bring forth one of the greatest prophets of Israel. Similarly, John the Baptist was not Zacharias's or Elizabeth's idea even though they were crying out for a child as well. He was the Lord's idea. It was God's plan for the one crying out in the wilderness, "Make ready the way of the Lord, make His paths straight!" (Matt. 3:3) to come forward.

The truth is that the promises of God (i.e., Samuel and John the Baptist) are not dependent upon your prayer life, but they are conceived through your prayer life. The groanings within you are placed there by God through your intimacy with Him. They are the very things He wants to accomplish through you, because you were created for good works. (See Ephesians 2:10.) The reason that some of us haven't seen the manifestation or the fulfillment of the groaning within us is not because there is some weird, twisted motive present. (See James 4:3.) It's a timing issue.

God was not withholding John the Baptist from Zacharias and Elizabeth. There is a time to be born. The angel Gabriel came to Zacharias as he was performing the priestly duties at the temple and told Zacharias these words:

> Do not be afraid, Zacharias, *for your petition has been heard*, and your wife Elizabeth will bear you a son, and you will give him the name John. "You will have joy and gladness, and many will rejoice at his birth. "For he will be great in the sight of the Lord; and he will drink no wine or liquor, and he will be filled with the Holy Spirit while yet in his mother's womb. "And he will turn many of the sons of Israel back to the Lord their God. "It is he who will go *as a forerunner* before Him in the spirit and power of Elijah, *to turn the hearts of the fathers back to the children*, and the disobedient to the attitude of the righteous, so as to make ready a people prepared for the Lord (emphasis mine). Luke 1:13–17

When the angel told Zacharias that his petition had been heard, it wasn't because Zacharias and Elizabeth had prayed one hundred times. God heard them the first time...

Fumbling to understand and conceive of everything Gabriel had told him, Zacharias asked how he could know that these words were true since he was an old man and his wife was beyond the age of child bearing. Here is Gabriel's response:

> The angel answered and said to him, "I am Gabriel, who stands in the presence of God, and I have been sent to speak to you and to bring you this good news. And behold, you shall be silent and unable to speak until the day when these things take place, because you did not

believe my words, *which will be fulfilled in their proper time*" (emphasis mine).

Luke 1:19–20

Some things truly are a timing issue with God and as much as we say "God's timing is perfect;" it's true. It's not a cliché. He knows what He's doing. The truth is that sometimes the amount of waiting between the conception of the promise and the birth of it is greater than nine months. But the joy over the birth of what was promised is far greater than any amount of labor pains it took to bring it into being. (See John 16:21.)

The Unrighteous Judge

Indeed, Hannah's story is really no different from the woman Jesus refers to through a parable in Luke 18. Here's the complete account:

> Now He was telling them a parable to show that at all times they ought to pray and not to lose heart, saying, "In a certain city there was a judge who did not fear God and did not respect man. There was a widow in that city, and she kept coming to him, saying, 'Give me legal protection from my opponent.' For a while he was unwilling; but afterward he said to himself, 'Even though I do not fear God nor respect man, yet because this widow bothers me, I will give her legal protection, otherwise by continually coming she will wear me out.' And the Lord said, "Hear what the unrighteous judge said; now, will not God bring about justice for His elect who cry to Him day and night, and will He delay long over them? "I tell you that He will bring about justice for them quickly. However, when the Son of Man comes, will He find faith on the earth?"

Luke 18:1–8

The legal protection the widow wanted from her opponent was the groaning within her and she knew exactly who to go to for the answer. Jesus called her relentless pursuit and desperation "faith." And it's Jesus Himself who is directing us to pay attention to what the unrighteous judge said because God will bring about justice for His elect who cry to Him day and night in the same way He opened Hannah's womb who also cried to Him. Why? Because your prayers from a pure heart that are in agreement with *His will* have the ability to pull heaven down to earth.

Pay attention to your groanings. What are they saying? What is the desire of your heart? Thankfully, like Hannah and like the widow above, we know who to turn to for the answer. We know the One who placed the groaning within us and who has the ability to bring it to pass. Sadly, some people have groanings within them that they don't know how to answer. They are seeking answers in all the wrong places. They are thirsty and don't know how to quench it, because the truth is that so many people have been drinking from the wrong well for far too long.

A Date by a Well

As I had mentioned in a previous chapter, the story about the woman at the well or what others refer to as the story about the Samaritan woman is one of my favorite stories in the Bible. (See John 4.) There are many things happening at one time as this story unfolds. There are cultural no-nos being broken (Jews have no dealings with Samaritans [John 4:9]). There are invitations being handed out (John 4:10, 13–14). There is a discussion about water with greater implications than its molecular structure of H_2O. And a lifestyle is exposed (John 4:17–18).

It's a beautiful story because *it's personal* and because we once again see the reality of a father looking for his long lost daughter and a daughter desperately searching for the way home.

Wearied after His journey from Judea to the small town Sychar in Samaria, Jesus parks Himself against Jacob's well.

While His disciples had left Him to go purchase some food, a woman from Samaria arrives to draw water from the very well that had become the source of Jesus's rest. It may not have been the most comfortable recliner, but it's what they had back then. It's at this point and time that Jesus says to the woman, "Give Me a drink." And it's these four small words that sparked a conversation that would forever change not only the life of this woman but also the inhabitants of the city where she was from. Let's take a look at it in detail.

There came a woman of Samaria to draw water. Jesus said to her, "Give Me a drink." For His disciples had gone away into the city to buy food. Therefore the Samaritan woman said to Him, "How is it that You, being a Jew, ask me for a drink since I am a Samaritan woman?" (For Jews have no dealings with Samaritans.) Jesus answered and said to her, "If you knew the gift of God, and who it is who says to you, 'Give Me a drink,' you would have asked Him, and He would have given you living water." She said to Him, "Sir, You have nothing to draw with and the well is deep; where then do You get that living water? You are not greater than our father Jacob, are You, who gave us the well, and drank of it himself and his sons and his cattle?" Jesus answered and said to her, "Everyone who drinks of this water will thirst again; but whoever drinks of the water that I will give him shall never thirst; but the water that I will give him will become in him a well of water springing up to eternal life." The woman said to Him, "Sir, give me this water, so I will not be thirsty nor come all the way here to draw." He said to her, "Go, call your husband and come here." The woman answered and said, "I have no husband." Jesus said to her, "You have correctly said, 'I have no husband'; for you have had five husbands, and the one whom you now have is not your husband; this you have said truly."

John 4:7–18

As I had mentioned earlier, the conversation between Jesus and this woman concerning water has absolutely nothing to do *with water* (I'll explain as we go along). When Jesus tells her to give Him a drink, He essentially wants this woman to see that she has nothing to give within herself and that He has everything to give. She has nothing to give because of where it is she has been drinking from. But He has everything to give because of what's inside of Him and because of who gave Him the authority to give it. (See John 5:26; 10:10.)

If the conversation isn't about water, what is it about? It's about where this woman was drawing her identity and significance from. It had nothing to do with the water that was within the well. It had to do with what was filling her heart. It had to do with what she thought was the answer and what she was drinking from that never satisfied—men. This is why Jesus said to her, "Go, call your husband and come here." He knew where she was drinking from.

There is no life in believing that people are the answer. This is why Jesus is asking this woman for a drink. He was fully aware of what she was caught up in and He knew she had nothing to give. She had five husbands, and the man she was now with wasn't her husband. If she didn't think men were the answer, she wouldn't have been on her sixth one.

Despite Jesus's knowledge about her lifestyle, He never used it against her. He never weighed her through it or condemned her because of it. Rather, He invited her into what He possessed. The gift of repentance was spread out upon His banqueting table for the woman to come and partake of. You can't say no to something without knowing what to say yes to. On one hand, the water within the well represented the well of men she had been drinking from. The water He offered, the well that springs up to eternal life, would quench her thirst and end her search.

When the women tells Jesus that the well is deep and that He has nothing to draw with (John 4:11), she is not saying that the water within the well is deep. No, she is explaining that the distance between the top of the well to where the water resides is deep. The chasm is deep. The space between is deep. If it wasn't, Jesus could have reached His hand down into the well and lapped up as much water as He wanted. But as I said earlier, this isn't your ordinary conversation about the benefits of drinking eight eight-ounce glasses of water a day. Jesus was revealing the correlation between the shallowness of the water within the well to the shallowness of what filled this woman's soul.

The reason that the well was deep is because people had to consistently return to it for water. Similarly, the well within the woman was deep because every man she turned to was another bucket of water from her own soul. The more she thought they were the answer, the more of her value and identity she gave away. All she was left with was thirst, which is why Jesus says to her, "Everyone who drinks of this water will thirst again." That's a promise, folks. Jesus doesn't lie.

The truth is that when we treat people like wells full of water, we move on to the next one once the well is dry. That's how survival works. You move on to where you think the source of life is. You need water to live. But we need to be sure we are drinking from the right place. In fact, I believe that whenever people wind up angry, bitter, frustrated, and disappointed with one another, it reveals that they had been trying to find who they are *in* and *through* one another. The well ran dry and because these people have nothing more to give, you look for another watering source. This is why marriages end and relationships crumble. What we are ultimately declaring is "I don't need you anymore. I've gotten everything I could from you. The need has been met and I'm moving on."

The fact that the water runs dry reveals that people, or anything else other than Jesus for that matter, can never be the answer. He's the only one who can give you living water that will become inside of you a well springing up to eternal life. And I can promise you that you want to drink from that well He's placed within you. It's where He lives and where His kingdom resides. (See John 14:23 and Luke 12:32.) It's where fellowship takes place and where the knowledge of Him abounds because the Holy Spirit leads you and guides you into all truth and brings to remembrance all that Jesus has said to us. (See John 14:26, 16:13.)

When Jesus says to the woman, "If you knew the gift of God, and *who it is* who says to you, 'Give Me a drink,' you would have asked Him, and He would have given you living water" (John 4:10), He reveals a very important point. The truth is that many of us did not know who He was. We more than likely never would have done what we did had we known Him. In fact, we've known everything else but Him. Life was our teacher, and it was designed to keep us from the knowledge of Him. We've known the pain of our past and the rejection of friends and family. We've fellowshipped with what the world has told us was the answer. We've sought to find ourselves through what we've owned and who we've been with. We've tried every other well and the water within them but His.

And yet despite not knowing Him, He still offers the opportunity to every person He's created and every person who has ever rejected Him to drink freely from the life He offers. The way we have treated Him or responded to Him has never changed the way He treats us or responds to us. His hands are always open. The cup is always extended. The light has been left on. Come home; come and drink, because we can know Him now.

Inside this woman from Samaria was a groaning she did not know how to answer. It's the God responding mechanism within each and every person He has created. Because we were created by Him and for Him, we innately search for Him without realizing it. People are looking for the way home. As I mentioned earlier in this book, what people are doing ultimately reveals what they are looking for. The fact that this woman had five husbands and was with a man who wasn't her husband paints a picture of a little girl lost in a crowd, desperately looking for her parents.

She was lost, and she was looking but so was her Father.

Her groaning was answered through Jesus's invitation. Because she didn't know Him, she didn't know to come to Him.

It's simple, guys.

Let's keep it that way.

And when she found Him and He found her, she came alive. She was forgiven and she knew it… There was no guilt. There was no shame. There was no condemnation. She finally found the man she'd be spending eternity with. The One she was looking for never held what she did outside of the knowledge of Him against her. She knew the search was over, which is why she so enthusiastically and emphatically returned to her city to tell its inhabitants about what and who she found (John 4:28–29). And as this woman returned with the good news that found her, she had brought with her the answer to every person's groaning. She brought with her the One who told her all the things she had done, and despite her mishaps, He still invited her to drink.

Bethel Music artist and worship leader, Steffany Frizzell Gretzinger[2], spontaneously sang the following words one day while performing her song of worship "Closer." "You could love me more in a moment than other lovers could in a lifetime." What a wonderfully accurate depiction of what transpired between this woman from Samaria and Jesus. She had many lovers. She had five husbands, and the man she was currently with wasn't her husband. And yet despite the many men she had been with, Jesus did more for her in a moment than the many years with these other men could *not* do. He *loved* her. He didn't cherish what she could do for Him. He *loved* her. He wasn't in need of anything from her. He *loved* her.

He loved her through the time He spent with her. He loved her through His words. He loved her by not holding against her the wake of men that lay in her path. And He loved her by offering her what no other man could give her—eternal life.

Although we may not have had multiple spouses like this woman, I'm sure we had other lovers. The things we give ourselves to and believe to be the answer do not necessarily have to be people. Anyplace and anything that we seek to draw significance from is a lover. Work can be a lover. Your position in life can be a lover. The approval of man can be a lover. Drugs can be lovers. Hobbies can be lovers. And people can be as well.

We need to understand that God has chosen to treat us no differently than He did this woman. I love her story because I get *it*. I lived *it*. I may not have lived it the way she did, but I sought after things, gave myself to things, and believed those things to be my source of life.

We need to understand that we returned to various wells of all kinds while all the while depleting whatever was inside of them. Greater still, we need to grasp that in the midst of the coming and going, One took the time to sit down and rest from His journey of seeking and saving the lost to offer to us what we had been looking for the whole time. We are *that* important to Him.

He won't condemn you for where you've been drinking from. He merely wants to offer you the very thing you were supposed to be drinking from the beginning. He wants you home. He wants you alive. He wants you to accept what He freely gives. He can love you more in a moment than other lovers could in a lifetime. We must spend time with this reality until it becomes our reality.

The Okay Corral
of the Gospel

Regarding Zion, I can't keep my mouth shut, regarding Jerusalem, I can't hold my tongue, until her righteousness blazes down like the sun and her salvation flames up like a torch.

Foreign countries will see your righteousness, and world leaders your glory. You'll get a brand-new name straight from the mouth of GOD. You'll be a stunning crown in the palm of GOD's hand, a jeweled gold cup held high in the hand of your God. No more will anyone call you Rejected, and your country will no more be called Ruined. You'll be called Hephzibah (My Delight), and your land Beulah (Married), Because GOD delights in you and your land will be like a wedding celebration. For as a young man marries his virgin bride, so your builder marries you, And as a bridegroom is happy in his bride, so your God is happy with you.

—Isaiah 62 (The Message)

BRIAN CONNOLLY

I Am Hephzibah
by Julie Meyer[1]

I am Hephzibah
I am Your delight
I am Hephzibah
The one that You love (repeat)

For I am Yours and You are mine
And we'll be together far beyond the boundary of time
And Your desire is for me and mine
Mine in for You
Mine is for You

I am clean, free, washed
Washed in the Blood of the Lamb
I am clean, free, washed
Washed in the Blood of Jesus
I am clean, free, washed
Washed in the Blood of the Lamb
I am clean, free, washed
Washed in the Blood of Jesus

It's my name,
It's my name
This is who I am

It's my name,
It's my name
This is who I am
This is who I am

It's my name
It's my name
Hephzibah

Clothed and Very Ashamed

Lt. Col. William C. Howey of the United States Marine Corps. This was the name of my tenth grade Social Studies teacher at Boyertown Area Senior High School. He was an amazing man. He was a great teacher. And he was one of my favorites.

This man had been to hell and back after serving three tours in Vietnam. He would tell my class stories about his time there. They were shocking and raw, and we ate them up. Every tenth grade boy lived for stories like the ones he would tell. He told us things he never told his family. He talked about the different forms of torture the Vietcong would employ upon American soldiers. He told stories about near-death experiences and how the longest amount of time he went without sleep was for two weeks. (I'm not even sure that's medically possible, but I do know the fear of what they were up against caused a lot of those boys to be sleep deprived.)

I don't know how else to say it. This dude was intense! This dude was real! It was as if we were learning from John Rambo himself. The only things that were missing were a red headband tied around his head, a submachine gun tucked under his arm pit, and a sash of bullets draped across his chest. But after thirty-two years of service in the military, Lt. Col. Howey settled behind a desk in a classroom in small town Boyertown, Pennsylvania, to teach a bunch of teenagers. I thought that was awesome.

One of the things we students had to do for Lt. Col. Howey's class was a lengthy report on various countries he'd assign to us. We had to research information on our assigned country and then give an oral report on our discoveries. We would have to report on such things as the country's population size, economy, resources, culture, etc. Lucky for me (not really), I was assigned the country of Japan. Let's just say that I had no idea how much there was to learn about Japan. Let's just say that I had no idea that my paper would wind up being a whopping eighteen pages long, which to this day is still one of the longest papers I have ever written for a class, and I have a masters degree!

Now, as I mentioned earlier, we not only had to write a paper, we had to give a report on it. Basically, each student stood in front of his or her peers and read their research paper verbatim. It was long. It was tedious. It was so boring! I wanted to hear stories about Vietnam, not sit and listen to my peers read about information I could have cared less about. I guess more than anything it was a good opportunity to catch up on any sleep you may have lost the night before.

When it finally came time for me to read my report, I was ready. Up to this very moment in time, I did not mind public speaking. I loved it. I felt like I was good at it. Whereas many people are more afraid of public speaking than they are of dying, I was comfortable standing in front of and exhorting my peers. But something was gravely different this time; something was off big time!

Everything was fine and dandy while reading the first nine out of eighteen pages. It felt like a breeze! I had hardly even noticed how quickly the time was passing, and then *it* happened. I instantly became aware that I still had nine more pages to read. I was only half the way finished and for some reason, I panicked. I freaked out on the inside, and I began to experience something that I had never experienced before in the realm of public speaking. I could hardly breathe. It was the strangest thing. I could breathe in, but I couldn't breathe out. As a result, my voice would crack and shake. My hands shook along with my voice. And then someone turned on the sweat machine. I began to sweat from my brow and would have to occasionally wipe it away with my free hand. I was so self-conscious in that moment it was ridiculous. I could feel the eyes of my peers as they looked on in horror. I could hear their smirks and laughter. And I could sense that I would never hear the end of this for a very long time.

Straight up, I was embarrassed. I was ashamed. And it took me many, many years to get over the fear of public speaking. I always find it comical that my area of greatest strength was terribly assaulted my sophomore year in high school. I remember trying to avoid every college and seminary class that involved oral presentations. I saw them as the plague. I wanted nothing to do with them. But the reality is that you can only run away from them for so long in your scholastic career. I was forced to bump into them along the way and every time I did, I would pray for *hours* before having to present. I would even write scripture passages on my papers about casting my anxiety on God and remembering that He was with me. It really wasn't until the end of 2009 that the boldness of God through the Holy Spirit came upon me to preach that the power that anxiety had in the realm of public speaking was finally broken off of me. Until that boldness came, I lived with that fear and that fear was the product of a lie that said, "You are going to blow it. You are going to look stupid. You are going to fail. Remember tenth grade?" I lived for nearly fourteen years with that yak-yak in my head and the fear that followed it.

Thank God for the Gospel! Thank God for truth that makes us free!

Despite the shame and embarrassment I felt as a young teenager, there's yet another woman's story in the Bible that far trumps my story. I honestly can't imagine how this young lady would have felt. I've tried to put myself in her shoes, but I still don't think I'm able to fully grasp the embarrassment, guilt, shame, and condemnation this woman would have felt in such a short amount of time. Her story is one that God had me preach for the entire year of 2012. And the more I preached it, the bigger and more amazing the story became.

Naked and Very, Very Ashamed

As we look at this woman's story together, I'm going to do something different this time. We'll read a verse or two together and then we will unpack what it is we read. We will stop and go along the way, all the while gaining revelation and a greater understanding of God's grace and mercy and the heartbeat of the Father. Ready? Let's go.

"Early in the morning He (Jesus) came again into the temple, and all the people were coming to Him; and He sat down and *began* to teach them" (John 8:2). The first thing we ought to take notice of is that Jesus is in the temple and the people were gathering to Him to hear Him teach. This is a public setting with many, many people. This wasn't a closed, exclusive group. The hungry and the thirsty came as well as those who were envious of Him and His following and those who would try to trap Him and humiliate Him publicly.

"The scribes and the Pharisees brought a woman caught in adultery, and having set her in the center *of the court*, they said to Him, 'Teacher, this woman has been caught in adultery, in the very act'" (John 8:3–4). If Jesus was going to judge this woman, this would have been the place to do it—in the center of the court, in front of the jury of onlookers and spectators! The scribes and Pharisees didn't just bring a woman who had previously committed adultery. They brought a woman caught in the very act! Don't miss this, guys. These scribes and Pharisees didn't hear about this woman's escapades through the rumor mill. Pharisee Joe didn't tell Scribe Bob something he heard one day about this woman so they could hold a counsel with the other scribes and Pharisees and later decide to bring the woman in for questioning. There was no interrogation. There was no lamp to place her under to make her sweat until she confessed. No. Someone had laid in wait to catch this woman in the very act. Not only that. Whomever it was that caught her did not leave her any time to dress herself. They brought her directly to the center of the court, the place where Jesus was, while in the midst of what she was caught in. And not only is she naked and on display in the physical sense, she's also naked and on display with her sin completely exposed. What she was experiencing in that moment was *not* what Adam and Eve experienced with God or one another in the garden (naked and not ashamed [Genesis 2:25]). The shame of that moment must have been crushing.

"Now in the Law Moses commanded us to stone such women; what then do You say?" (John 8:5). This question from the scribes and Pharisees to Jesus wasn't unfounded. It had merit, but the motive behind it was wrong. Leviticus 20:10 does mention that if a man commits adultery with another man's wife, both the adulterer and adulteress should be put to death. It is in the law of Moses, but the questioners weren't seeking understanding. They weren't looking for answers. They were seeking to humiliate the One they were asking. They were looking for a way to trap Jesus and stone Him with their words.

What I find fascinating at this point and time during the story is that the woman is in the center of the court without her partner in crime. Somehow the man got away scot-free, which leads me to wonder if perhaps it was not the man she was with that was married. Maybe she was the one who was married since her absentee lover vanished without a trace. If she were married, she would have had nowhere to run or hide. She was exposed.

The Wyatt Earp of the Gospel

"They were saying this, testing Him, so that they might have grounds for accusing Him. But Jesus stooped down and with His finger wrote on the ground" (John 8:6). This very scene that was just described to you in verse 6 is what I like to refer to as the "Okay Corral of the Gospel." It's the showdown between love that sees the value of the person and judgment of the flesh based on performance. Although the scribes and Pharisees didn't bring guns to the temple for a shootout, they did bring something else. They brought stones, and behind their stones were hearts full of judgment, eyes that could only see what the woman did (behavior) and not who she was (value), and a motive to make Jesus look like a fool. In all honesty, they brought with them everything they learned through the fall of man and their very heart of stone.

In Genesis 3:7, it says that the eyes of Adam and Eve were opened. Unfortunately, the wrong sets of eyes were opened. As a result, we inherited the ability to judge one another by the flesh as opposed to love that covers a multitude of sin. (See 1 Peter 4:8.) We weighed ourselves and everyone else around us through the knowledge of good and evil. We became gods in our own right, and we lived like the brothers found in Luke 15—destroyed and full of self-pity when we did wrong (the younger brother) and puffed up and full of self-righteousness when we did right (the older brother). We marked people according to their behavior and presumed to know their motives. As a result, our hearts became hearts of stone and we needed God to make them hearts of flesh. (See Ezekiel 36:26.) In fact, it's rumored that when people such as this woman caught in adultery were stoned, the hurlers would use stones the size of a human heart. It's my belief that these accusers weren't armed with ordinary stones. They were armed with what was in their heart. They held within their hands what was protected by a cage of bones inside of them. They held the coldness and indifference of their own hearts.

They came with the very weapon that the accuser of the brethren (see Revelation 12:10) seeks to use against every Christian but was disempowered through the cross.

> When you were dead in your transgressions and the uncircumcision of your flesh, He made you alive together with Him, having forgiven us all our transgressions, *having canceled out the certificate of debt consisting of decrees against us, which was hostile to us*; and He has taken it out of the way, having nailed it to the cross. When He had disarmed the rulers and authorities, He made a public display of them, having triumphed over them through Him (emphasis mine).
>
> Colossians 2:13–15

They came demanding payment. They wanted retribution. And as much as this woman was on trial before every on looking eye, the Pharisees and scribes were utilizing the weakness of this woman's flesh to back Jesus into a corner, thus, putting Him on trial as well. They didn't like how He did things and they viewed Him as a threat to the power they occupied over the people and the glory they received from one another. (See John 5:44.) They loved the approval of men, and they were losing it because of the ones who were coming to believe in Jesus. (See John 12:43.) But mercy triumphs over judgment (see James 2:13), and you can't trap truth. You either allow it to set you free or you reject it with a hardened heart. And Jesus was fully aware of what was in men during His ministry on the earth. (See John 2:24–25.) He knew the motive behind what the Pharisees and scribes were doing and He still took a nail for them. He never allowed their heart toward Him affect His heart toward them. He loved them.

The Ministry of Condemnation Versus the Ministry of Righteousness

"But when they persisted in asking Him, He straightened up, and said to them, "He who is without sin among you, let him *be the* first to throw a stone at her." Again He stooped down and wrote on the ground" (John 8:7–8).

I've heard many interesting commentaries concerning what it was that Jesus wrote on the ground and why it is that He stooped down to write it to begin with. I've heard people say that He was writing on the ground the sins of those who brought the woman before Him. I've heard people say that He was drawing a line in the sand to determine if people were for Him or against Him. I've heard people say that no one knows for sure what He wrote or why He wrote it. But I believe that there is nothing written in the scriptures by happenstance. I do not think that God is "filling space" with useless words. Things are written for a reason and I believe that the reason He stooped down to write on the ground is because the very law that the accusers are using to promote their case for stoning this adulteress is the very law He wrote with His own finger. (See Exodus 31:18.) Why is this significant? It's significant because Jesus didn't come to judge the world but to save it. (See John 3:17.) It's significant because Jesus didn't come to count men's trespasses against them (see 2 Corinthians 5:19) but to remove them. In other words, Jesus wasn't armed with the ministry of condemnation. He was armed with the ministry of righteousness. Jesus was writing a new law in the ground, the law of the spirit of life. (Romans 8:2.)

Jesus had to write on the ground because the ministry of condemnation that had glory was fading and a new ministry was about to be instituted.

> But if the ministry of death, in letters engraved on stones, came with glory, so that the sons of Israel could not look intently at the face of Moses because of the glory of his face, fading *as* it was, how will the ministry of the Spirit fail to be even more with glory? For if the ministry of condemnation has glory, much more does the ministry of righteousness abound in glory. For indeed what had glory, in this case has no glory because of the glory that surpasses *it*. For if that which fades away *was* with glory, much more that which remains *is* in glory.
>
> 2 Corinthians 3:7–11

The ministry of condemnation can only value you based on your ability to keep the law. Like a mirror, it can only show you your reflection. It shows when you're doing right and when you're doing wrong, but it can never change you or cleanse you. It can only value your performance and yet righteousness was never to be attained through it. Righteousness can only come by faith. (See Romans 3 and 4.) The law was to tutor you to Christ, to show you your need for a savior. (See Galatians 3:24.) And the Law wasn't going to save this woman who had been brought before the feet of Jesus, naked and ashamed. She didn't need to be told what she did wrong. She was fully aware of what she did. The only thing that was going to change her was the understanding and love she was about to see in the eyes of the One that created her.

Bill Johnson,[2] senior pastor of Bethel Church in Redding, California, says that this is a moment in time between a father and his daughter. It was a moment where a father was about to pardon his daughter and welcome her back into the fold. It was a moment where a father was about to look into the eyes of his most prized possession and say with one glimpse, "I love you." It was a moment where a daughter was about to find in her father what she was looking for in the arms a of the person she was with and caught in. It was a moment where a daughter was about to be treated in way she did not expect.

Condemnation wants to stone you. Righteousness wants to clothe you.

The ministry of righteousness values the person, not their behavior. The ministry of righteousness uses righteous judgment. It's full of understanding. It knows why people do what they do and that if they could only see what God sees, they wouldn't be doing what they are doing. If this adulteress fully understood the love of God and who her Father was, she wouldn't have been caught doing the unthinkable. The law wasn't going to set her straight. Judgment wasn't going to change her. Only the mercy and kindness of God could do that.

> For what the Law could not do, weak as it was through the flesh, God *did*: sending His own Son in the likeness of sinful flesh and *as an offering* for sin, He condemned sin in the flesh, so that the requirement of the Law might be fulfilled in us, who do not walk according to the flesh but according to the Spirit.
>
> Romans 8:3–4

Put Down Your Weapons

"When they heard it, they *began* to go out one by one, beginning with the older ones, and He was left alone, and the woman, where she was, in the center *of the court*" (John 8:9). What did they, the ones who brought this woman before Jesus in an effort to test Him, hear? What does that mean when John writes, "When they heard 'it'"? What is "*it*"? Is "it" what Jesus said, "He who is without sin among you, let him *be the* first to throw a stone at her."? If "it" was what Jesus said to them, why wouldn't we read something like, "When they heard what Jesus said"? That would make a whole lot of sense, wouldn't it? I mean that's what normal people would have written, right? Maybe what they heard *was* the indictment Jesus brought against their own judgment and attempt to trap Him when He disarmed the stones they were carrying by revealing that they too were without sin. Maybe "it" was the charge against them.

Maybe.

But what if the source of the sound was not found in what Jesus said but was found in what *He did*. What if the sound actually came from what He wrote in the ground? What if what these Pharisees and scribes heard was the end of one ministry and the beginning of another? If the finger of God had written the law on the tablets of stone, perhaps these men were hearing the etching of a new law—a law where righteousness wouldn't be dependent on our ability to keep the Law but rather on His ability to keep it and fulfill what we couldn't so that righteousness would be established through faith in the finished work of Jesus. Please understand that I am in no way shape or form negating the Law and claiming it doesn't exist. Jesus Himself said that He did not come to abolish the Law or the prophets but to fulfill them and that not the smallest letter or stroke of the Law shall pass until heaven and earth pass away and until all is accomplished. (See Matthew 5:17–18.) The Law is holy and righteous and good (see Romans 7:12), but it could never perfect or cleanse my conscience from dead works. (See Hebrews 9:9, 10:1.) All the Law could do, however, was make me conscious of my sin. It was never the answer to sin. What I'm saying is a new covenant was about to be instituted through the shed blood of Jesus Christ, a covenant where the following verses would become a reality.

> "This is the covenant that I will make with them after those days, says the Lord: I will put my laws upon their heart, and on their mind I will write them," *He then says,* "and their sins and their lawless deeds I will remember no more."
>
> Hebrews 10:16–17

I no longer live according to the letter of the Law. I do, however, live by the Spirit of it. As a result, you become a living expression of the law because your heart has changed. You begin to love from a pure place as opposed to a selfish one. Your very life becomes a letter that people read in the same way that Moses read the Ten Commandments on the tablets of stone to the Israelites. The word becomes flesh within you. You become a living expression of Jesus for all to see. Your very life may be the only Bible someone ever reads. This is why Paul writes the following words to the Corinthians.

> You are our letter, written in our hearts, known and read by all men; being manifested that you are a letter of Christ, cared for by us, written not with ink but with the Spirit of the living God, not on tablets of stone but on tablets of human hearts.
>
> 2 Corinthians 3:2–3

Also, righteousness (my right standing with God) would no longer be established through my external ability to follow the Law. It would become an inward reality as a result of grace through faith. It would be the laws of God written upon my heart and mind. It would be based upon His doing, not my doing. It's His good pleasure to grant us such a gift. He doesn't want your salvation or standing with Him to be based on your works so that none of us would boast in our own ability. (See Ephesians 2:8–9.)

This is why I believe that these Pharisees and scribes were hearing a changing of the guard. I believe that everything God does comes through a sound and that we need to have ears to hear and eyes to see what the Lord is doing. Amos 3:7 reveals that God does nothing without revealing His secret counsel to the prophets. That means that someone has to first hear and then speak. When you hear, you can see. Jesus only spoke what He heard spoken to Him directly from His Father. (See John 12:49–50.) Let's not forget that God *spoke* creation into existence. Sound precedes "being."

> For the promise to Abraham or to his descendants that he would be heir of the world was not through the Law, but through the righteousness of faith. For if those who are of the Law are heirs, faith is made void and the promise is nullified; for the Law brings about wrath, but where there is no law, there also is no violation. For this reason *it is* by faith, in order that *it may be* in accordance with grace, so that the promise will be guaranteed to all the descendants, not only to those who are of the Law, but also to those who are of the faith of Abraham, who is the father of us all, (as it is written, "*A father of many nations have I made you*") in the presence of Him whom he believed, *even* God, who gives life to the dead *and calls into being that which does not exist* (emphasis mine).
>
> Romans 4:13–17

Clothed and Not Ashamed

"Straightening up, Jesus said to her, 'Woman, where are they? Did no one condemn you?' She said, 'No one, Lord.' And Jesus said, 'I do not condemn you, either. Go. From now on sin no more'" (John 8:10–11).

This story began at the center of the court and ends at the center of the court. Although the writer is describing the geographic location of this moment, I like to view the "center of the court" as the place where judgment is about to be decreed. It's in the court of law where verdicts are read. If judgment is going to be rendered, it's going to be now, here, *in the center of the court*. And what was the judgment that was given? "I do not condemn you either."

The knowledge of what a person did wrong leaves them naked and ashamed, but it is love that covers a multitude of sin. (See 1 Peter 4:8.) Nothing clothes you or sets you free from the consciousness of sin like, "I do not condemn you either." It's the word that makes us clean. (See John 15:3 and Ephesians 5:26.) And with six simple words, Jesus removed the shame of this woman by clothing her nakedness (the realization of her sin) with truth. Those six words that were spirit and life instantly restored to that woman what her accusers tried to take away.

"I do not condemn you either" is the greatest garment we could ever wear. You can try to put on the garment of the acceptance of men or the garment of performance or hide behind the garment of addictions, but those garments will always wear out. That's why you have to keep doing what you're doing in order to patch up your garment. But no one puts a new piece of cloth on an old garment because he would also tear the new and it would not match the old. (See Luke 5:36.) You need to take off your old garments—your identity of everything you were and did before Christ came. The only garment that fits you now is the garment of His love and mercy and the fact that He has made you His own. Just like the father did with the younger brother upon his return in Luke 15, your Father has placed a robe around your shoulders, a ring upon your finger, and sandals on your feet. You're home.

God does not want you living in the shame of your past. He never wants the mistakes you made as a result of wrong believing to be the eye you see yourself through. In fact, after Adam and Eve sinned and realized they were naked, God fashioned garments for them out of the skin of an animal. (See Genesis 3:21.) Why? Because fig leaves will eventually wear out. A leaf can only cover you for so long before it withers and exposes the thing you were hiding, and every withering leaf would leave behind the constant reminder of what they did wrong and how they blew it. It's no different than the sacrifices that were offered through the Law.

"But in those *sacrifices* there is a reminder of sins year by year" (Heb. 10:3).

There were no sacrifices that this adulteress could have offered that would have taken away the consciousness of what she did wrong. They would have forever left her naked in the shame of the act she was caught in and would have reminded her over and over again that she blew it. The only thing that would be effectual enough would be the pardoning words of her God. And the only garment that wouldn't wear out would be the garment of righteousness that wouldn't be based on her ability to clean up her act but based on the finished work of the cross. It's a faith thing, not a performance thing. It's a gift freely given, but it is also a gift that must be received.

Whether this found daughter of the King realized it or not in the moment, she would have one day come to the knowledge that the One who gazed in her eyes and did not condemn her was the same person who knew who she was before she was ever created. She would have one day understood that the One who created it all and upholds all things by the word of His power (see Hebrews 1:3) still spoke her name and called her into existence knowing full well that He would one day be face–to–face with her in her darkest hour. She would have known one day that she looked into the eyes of her God and heard the forgiving words of her Savior. And that, dear readers, would leave her forever changed. She is Hephzibah. She is His delight. She is the one that He loves. But then again, we all are.

That's why she could go from that place and sin no more. You can't do the second without the first. The forgiveness of sin is the answer to the power of sin. Where sin increased, grace abounded all the more. (See Romans 5:20.)

"Are we to continue in sin so that grace may increase? May it never be! How shall we who died to sin still live in it?" (Rom. 6:1–2).

Grace isn't the empowerment to sin; it's the *answer* to sin.

> For the grace of God has appeared, bringing salvation to all men, instructing us to deny ungodliness and worldly desires and to live sensibly, righteously and godly in the present age, looking for the blessed hope and the appearing of the glory of our great God and Savior, Christ Jesus, who gave Himself for us to redeem us from every lawless deed, and to purify for Himself a people for His own possession, zealous for good deeds.
>
> Titus 2:11–14

How can you continue in something you died to? You continue in it when you don't understand what this woman found through the grace filled words of Jesus. It's His grace that empowers me to do the very things Paul writes about to Titus in the verses above. His grace causes me to want to live godly. Why? Because when I see and understand verse 14, namely that He redeemed me from every lawless deed, I want to give myself to Him and become just like Him. I want to live for what He did on my behalf. When I believe in His love for me I become zealous for good deeds. The fact that you keep His commandments is the evidence that you love Him.

"He who has My commandments and keeps them is the one who loves Me" (John 14:21).

It would have been impossible for this woman to keep the command of, "Go. From now on sin no more" without encountering the mercy, forgiveness, and grace of God. The experience with such things creates a love within me for Him and causes me to want to watch over and guard His commandments. We love, after all, because He first loved us (1 John 4:19).

But how do we come to understand in a greater way the things that these women experienced in these last three chapters? What causes the light to come on in a greater way? How do we take off the garments of our past and put on who we are in Christ? How do we grow in the understanding of our forgiveness? Now that we've been brought face-to-face with the fact that we want to know God and the beauty of His gospel in a better way, where do we go from here? We will unpack the answers to these questions in the next three chapters, which could quite possibly be the most important chapters you read in this book.

You Can Have *It* Too

If you tell me this, I'll tell you how spiritual you are: will you tell me how much you pray? Brother, I'm not interested if you're booked up ten years; I'm not concerned about how many books you've read, how many doctorates you have or how large your church is, tell me how much you pray!

No man is greater than his prayer life. The pastor who is not praying is playing; the people who are not praying are straying. We have many organizers, but few agonizers; many players and payers, few prayers; many singers, few clingers; lots of pastors, few wrestlers; many fears, few tears; much fashion, little passion; many interferers, few intercessors; many writers, but few fighters. Failing here, we fail everywhere.

The secret of praying is praying in secret.

—Leonard Ravenhill[1]

"But you, when you pray, go into your inner room, close your door and pray to your Father who is in secret, and your Father who sees *what is done* in secret will reward you" (Matt. 6:6).

Get Off the Stage

I recently had the honor of being the guest speaker for an event at Gateway Fellowship in Seaford, Delaware, called "Fresh

Encounter 3." This was my second time being asked to be the featured speaker for these events. I also had the privilege of preaching at "Fresh Encounter 2" last year. I guess I must have done something right to have been asked back! In all seriousness, though, I absolutely love what God is doing at Gateway Fellowship and I'm amazed that He used me in such a way last year and this year to continue to fan into flame the gift of God within them. (See 2 Timothy 1:6.)

What happened last year is difficult to describe. The congregation was exposed to certain things for the first time that resulted in what I would describe as a bomb going off in their midst. They learned more about the love of God and encountered it as well. It's not that they didn't *know about* the love of God; it's that God opened their heart to receive what their head had been storing up for years and years. Knowledge became experience. They learned about their identity in Christ and how it's possible to not carry around offense, to live a life of love so as to not be in need of or offended by others. (See 1 John 2:10.) And they had both heard and experienced the biblical foundation for the baptism of the Spirit during our final night together.

Indeed, the testimonies from that November 16–18 weekend were profound, heart-warming, and life changing. The people in attendance noticed a radical difference within their own lives immediately. The light came on in a greater way, and they were lit on fire by and for God. I love when God does things like that. One of my most favorite things to do is to teach on the baptism of the Spirit and pray for others to receive it. It's beautiful. I thoroughly enjoy watching people become more aware of God and walk away with a greater desire to worship, live holy, and to love the Lord their God and their neighbor as themselves.

Truthfully, I wanted God to repeat at this most recent Fresh Encounter what He did during last year's Fresh Encounter. But that's not what He had in mind and I'm finding that it's a much greater idea to follow Him than to try to get Him to follow you!

During the last night of the event, I had spoken about what it means to be desperate in prayer and to hunger after God (this is an idea that I will develop in the last chapter). At the end of the message, I had given everyone an opportunity to bring their desperation and hunger to the altar and to cry out to God. It was powerful. The Holy Spirit began to brood over the people and their cries began to rise to heaven. People began weeping as a spirit of repentance had entered the meeting. We began asking for forgiveness for our saying one thing with our mouths and another with our lives. We repented for our unbelief and asked God to grant us the capacity to love the way He loves and to have a heart for the lost. People groaned before the presence of God. Even I was glued to the floor in a prostrate position with tears flowing from my eyes. It was during this time that I heard God say something to me that I had never heard before. I heard Him say, "Get off the stage. It's not about you. This is between Me and them now. I don't want them looking to you. Don't pray for any of them."

The truth is that I wanted to pray for every single person that flooded that altar. I wanted to lay my hands on as many as were hungry and thirsty, but God had other plans. The moment He spoke those words to me, I picked myself up off the ground, tiptoed around the people so as to not step on any of them, walked to the back of the sanctuary and told my friend who had come with me, "Let's go. We're out of here. I'm done." Truthfully, it felt weird vanishing like that without an explanation, but I would rather obey God than disobey.

The next day, I had the honor of bringing the event to a close by preaching at their Sunday morning worship service. Before taking the stage, a dear, sweet elder from the church named Dennis had approached me with tears in his eyes and with trembling and said, "God is saying to be ready to shift and move." His very words were the confirmation I needed for what happened the night before. They also brought validity for the direction I believed God was leading me in for that morning as well.

Sadly, I believe that one of the things we have done within the body of Christ is that we have "celebritized" certain ministers. It's as if we've left and walked away from the celebrities of the world only to make celebrities out of the people God calls grace gifts to men. (See Ephesians 4:7–16.) The whole purpose of the apostle, prophet, evangelist, pastor, and teacher is "for the equipping of the saints for the work of service, to the building up of the body of Christ; until we all attain to the unity of the faith, and of the knowledge of the Son of God, to a mature man, to the measure of the stature which belongs to the fullness of Christ" (Eph. 4:12–13).

We were never meant to regard them as anomalies. The grace that is upon them exists so that it might be reproduced in us. They exist so that we can walk in what they walk in.

There's a difference between uniformity and unity. We don't all have to look the same and talk the same, but we can agree on why it is that we woke up this morning—to manifest Christ. The unity of the faith is a byproduct of the apostles, prophets, evangelists, pastors, and teachers equipping us and sowing into our lives so that we may look more and more like Christ every day. As a result, the greatest anointing should not rest upon any one individual; rather, it should reside within the body of Christ.

"Behold, how good and how pleasant it is for brothers to dwell together in unity! It is like the precious oil upon the head, coming down upon the beard, *Even* Aaron's beard, coming down upon the edge of his robes" (Ps. 133:1–2).

As we attain to the unity of the faith, knowing who we are and why we are, we will walk in the same grace that God pours out upon those who exist to equip us and help us mature. The greatest concentration of the precious oil God pours out upon the apostles, prophets, evangelists, pastors, and teachers does not reside upon their heads. It's poured out upon us through them, collecting at the edge of the robes.

I believe God had Dennis tell me that it's time to shift and move because the leaders need to begin to *shift* the power to the people (if I can say it that way) and *move* out of the way. The body of Christ doesn't need celebrities. It needs people who understand that the goal of our instruction is love. (See 1 Timothy 1:5.) We need people to understand who they are and whose they are. If leaders only point people to themselves and never into the arms of Jesus, they have failed. The goal is that they'd multiply what is within them into the rest of us, not lead people into believing that they are in constant need of ministry. In fact, I believe we have a ministry crazed culture. I believe we have failed to help people understand that they have been ministered to through the finished work of Christ. Rather than helping people to put on the full armor of Christ, we've caused them to believe that there is always something lacking within them.

Just the other day, I was meditating on what God had told Adam after He created him in His image. In Genesis 1:28, God tells Adam to be fruitful and to multiply. It was during this time that God helped me to see that my four daughters are greater than just one of me. If God can take what is within their father and reproduce it within them, they will be far more effective. Why? Four is greater than one. The same principle applies to any congregation of believers. A congregation of believers is greater in number and effectiveness than one pastor. I believe the problem is that we have failed to some extent to see this. We are more busy running to be ministered to than growing in the faith.

Some people might argue that the reason I am the way I am is because of the grace that rests upon me from God as one of His grace gifts to men. As true as that might be, I can promise you that the revelation and understanding I walk in and the life I live is the result of my seeking Him in secret. I am the way I am because I want to know Him. We must help others within the body of Christ to understand this. What I have, you can have. The question that needs answered is, How desperate are you to find it? How thirsty are you? How hungry are you? In John 7:37–38, Jesus says, "Now on the last day, the great *day* of the feast, Jesus stood and cried out, saying, 'If anyone is thirsty, let him *come to Me* and drink. He who believes in Me, as the Scripture said, 'From his innermost being will flow rivers of living water'" (emphasis mine).

Although Jesus is referring to the baptism of the Holy Spirit, the principle I am seeking to draw from His words is the same nonetheless. The reality is that Jesus is asking us to come to Him. "Come to *Me*," He says. "Come to *Me*." He doesn't say that we should look here or there or run to and fro. He says, "Come to *Me*." It's one thing to have the groaning for more within you. It's another to know where to take it.

I remember Leonard Ravenhill[2] saying the following in one of his many sermons concerning prayer. Although I won't be able to quote him verbatim, you'll still be able to grab a hold of the point he was trying to make. One of the things he pointed out was that after Jesus had finished praying in a certain place, His disciples did not approach Him and say to Him, "Teach us how to preach." They said, "Teach us how to pray." (See Luke 11:1.) Leonard also pointed out that Paul never said, "Put on conferences at all times without ceasing." He said, "Pray without ceasing." (See 1 Thessalonians 5:17.) It's not wrong to want to be equipped to preach, and it's not wrong to go to conferences. I've had many wonderful experiences with both things. But the greatest thing you could ever do is cultivate a relationship with God and that comes through prayer. It's your personal God reality that will carry you through this life. It's the only thing that counts and it comes by knowing Him.

It's 4:20 Somewhere

In the first chapter of this book, I made mention of the fact that I believed God had wanted me to read the book of Acts at the beginning of 2013. I was not amazed by the many signs and wonders that God had performed in their midst and through the apostles. Don't get me wrong; I long to experience the things that are recorded in the book of Acts. But I was amazed by their boldness. I was shocked that they never cracked under pressure. They had joy in the direst of circumstances. They worshiped in the midst of imprisonments and gloried in their suffering for His name's sake. That's not something you accomplish on your own strength and will power. That's something that comes forth from the abundance of your heart, where all belief resides. They weren't biting their lips in an effort to not revile against those who were reviling them or to restrain themselves from striking the ones who struck them. There was something that was sown so deep within them that no trial, persecution, or worry could snatch it away, and I believe Acts 4:20 holds the key. It says, "We cannot stop speaking about what we have *seen and heard*" (Acts 4:20; emphasis mine).

Let me give you the context behind why it is that Peter and John made this statement. In Acts 3:1-8, Peter and John happen to stumble upon a man who had been lame from his mother's womb sitting at the gate called Beautiful just outside of the temple. Peter and John were heading to the temple because it was the hour of prayer, but this man was doing what he had always done for the greater part of the forty years he had been lame. He was begging.

When the man at the gate called Beautiful saw Peter and John, he began asking to receive mercy. Peter and John fixed their gaze upon him and said, "Look at us!" Why? Shame had held this man's head low for far too long. He lost sight of who he was. His condition identified him and Peter and John wanted to restore to him what forty years of being lame stole from him. The man began to give them his attention because he expected to receive something from them. Instead, Peter told the man that neither he nor John possessed silver or gold. They didn't have money. They had something far greater to give. They were born again. They were baptized in the Holy Spirit. And they had the name and authority of Jesus Christ, the Nazarene. What they freely received, they wanted to freely give and they told the man to walk. Peter seized the man by the hand and raised him up.

Immediately, the man's ankles and feet were strengthened and like a baby learning to walk for the first time, the man leapt and began walking and praising God.

Believe it or not, this miracle and what Peter and John were preaching to the people concerning the resurrection from the dead being found in Jesus greatly disturbed the priests, the captain of the temple guard and the Sadducees. (See Acts 4:1–2.) As a result, they laid hands on Peter and John and placed them in jail over night. On the next day, the "powers at be" began to question Peter and John about what power or in what name they healed the man at the gate called Beautiful. As simple as Peter could make it, he plainly explains that it was Jesus Christ the Nazarene—the One the rulers and elders and scribes had crucified and God raised from the dead—that had strengthened the man and had caused him to appear before all in good health.

After deliberating together, the council commanded Peter and John to no longer speak or teach at all in the name of Jesus. This is where we read in context the following words of Peter and John: "But Peter and John answered and said to them, 'Whether it is right in the sight of God to give heed to you rather than to God, you be the judge; for we cannot stop speaking about what we have seen and heard'" (Acts 4:19–20).

"For we cannot stop speaking."

There is a difference between *cannot* and *will not*. *Will not* requires your own strength, your own will. It's defiant. "I *will not* do that or I *won't* do that," someone might say. *Cannot* has nothing to do with you. It's beyond your control. Something else has taken you over. It wasn't up to them as to whether or not they were going to stop speaking about what they had seen and heard. They weren't being defiant or dishonoring toward the council. They literally had no choice in the matter. They were overtaken by what they experienced with Jesus and it controlled their very vocal chords. What poured forth in speech was the result of the abundance within their heart. When something is in abundance, it overflows. You can only fill a glass so high with water until it begins to pour over the rim. The glass has no choice. It can only contain so much liquid. It literally cannot stop releasing the contents it cannot hold. Similarly, Peter and John could not contain the rivers of living water pouring out from within them.

What they had seen and heard led to a man being healed in Acts 3. What they had seen and heard was the Word of Life, the One from the beginning. What they had seen and heard was the One the members of the council had recognized them as having been with.

"Now as they observed the confidence of Peter and John and understood that they were uneducated and untrained men, they were amazed, and *began* to recognize them as having been with Jesus" (Acts 4:13).

What they had seen and heard was relational. It led to their knowing the heart of God and the One who had come to seek and save them. Their knowing Jesus Christ resulted in great confidence and boldness before their accusers and a miracle performed on a man who had been lame for forty years. They knew the One who was for them and not against them. (See Romans 8:31.) They knew the One who was their advocate and who lived to make intercession for them. (See 1 John 2:1 and Hebrews 7:25.)

You Can Have It Too

Peter, John, and the rest of the boys were captivated by their experiences with Jesus. You couldn't shut them up. They were baptized into Christ and would never be the same as long as they lived. They would ultimately give their lives for the One who gave His life for them.

Could you imagine being alive at what Galatians 4:4 refers to as the "fullness of the time?" Could you imagine following the One who was the fulfillment of everything you ever heard about as a boy or girl growing up? Could you imagine being a part of the generation that would experience the things the prophets prophesied knowing that they weren't serving themselves and things into which angels long to look? (See 1 Peter 1:10–12.)

The truth is that we didn't miss our time to be born and everything that they had and experienced with Jesus is available to us. What I mean by that is even though you didn't know Jesus according to the flesh the way the disciples did even though you didn't hear His earthly voice or touch Him or see Him, you can have the same fellowship with Him as they did through the Holy Spirit. It would be very easy for us to sell ourselves short by concluding that because we weren't born two thousand years ago that there is no possible way that we could know Him in the same manner as those who walked with Him. Look at what 1 John 1:1–3 says concerning this idea.

> What was from the beginning, what we have heard, what we have seen with our eyes, what we have looked at and touched with our hands, concerning the Word of Life— and the life was manifested, and we have seen and testify and proclaim to you the eternal life, which was with the Father and was manifested to us—what we have seen and heard we proclaim to you also, so that you too may have fellowship with us; and indeed our fellowship is with the Father, and with His Son Jesus Christ.
>
> 1 John 1:1–3

Please don't misunderstand me. I would have loved to have been one of the disciples. I would have loved to have placed my head against His chest in the same way John did. (See John 13:23.) I would have loved to have been Thomas who was able to place his finger in the holes of His hands and take his hand and place it where the soldier's sword had pierced Him. (See John 20:27.) I would have loved to have been Peter who witnessed Jesus walking on the water and who attempted to do the same. (See Matthew 14:25–29.) I would have loved to have seen the countless multitudes fed and healed. And yet John is saying through three simple verses above that we can have the same fellowship with the Father and with Jesus that they all had.

Indeed, the verses above are John's way of saying, "I was there!" He touched Jesus with His hands. He saw Jesus with His eyes. And now he's calling us into the fellowship! He is proclaiming to us everything that he experienced so we can experience it too.

In Matthew 20:1–16, Jesus tells a parable about a landowner who went out early in the morning to hire laborers for his vineyard. The landowner agreed with the laborers to pay them a denarius for the day. Throughout various hours of the day, the landowner finds different people standing idle in the marketplace. He decides to hire these people as well to work in his vineyard and agrees to pay them the same amount as those he hired earlier that day. Some he hired at the third hour of the day. Others, he hired at the sixth and ninth hours. And then there were those he hired at the eleventh hour who would only work *one hour* and get paid the same as those who labored *all day.*

Come on now. Don't miss this. Put yourself in this parable. Could you imagine working all day and getting paid the same amount as those who worked for one hour? A denarius was a day's wage back then. Working one hour is not the same as working all day the last time I checked. But that's amazing grace, isn't it? And that's how the Lord does things. He's rich in mercy and full of grace. He shows no partiality to anyone. He loves us all unfailingly and equally.

In the introduction of this book, I referenced the story of Lazarus. (See John 11.) It's within this story that Jesus mentions that there are twelve hours in the day and that those who walk in the day do not stumble because they see the light of this world (John 11:9). There's obviously a very practical application to this verse in that when it's day and the sun is shining (the light of this world), I am less inclined to trip over things that would be hidden in the dark. But Jesus isn't talking about the sun and your sure footing, is He? No. He's talking about Himself. In John 8:12, Jesus calls Himself the Light of the World and makes mention that if anyone follows Him, they will not walk in the darkness, but will have the light of life. He's the truth and through Him, we see things for what they really are. He reveals the heart of the Father and what we were created to be and do from the beginning.

I believe that we, the body of Christ, are in the eleventh hour and are getting ready to step into the twelfth and final hour of the day. I believe we will see more and understand more and as we do, it will lead to a greater transformation of life and lives impacted around us. As we behold the Light, others will see the light within us.

"If I say, 'Surely the darkness will overwhelm me, And the light around me will be night,' Even the darkness is not dark to You, And the night is as bright as the day. Darkness and light are alike *to You*" (Ps. 139:11–12).

We will not be overwhelmed. The light around us will not become darkness. Like David who wrote this Psalm, we will have an increased revelation of who it is that formed our inward parts and wove us in our mother's womb. We will cherish His thoughts and His light will shine brightly through us and those sitting in darkness will behold a great light.

I say all of this because John is saying that we can have the same intimacy with Jesus that he enjoyed. I say all of this because if we really are in the eleventh hour, we will be given everything that was given to those who labored long before us. We can walk in and experience the very things John is calling us into. We can be paid the same amount as they were. We can walk in the same grace. And it is my personal opinion that these things are attained through intimacy and communion with God. If we want to have what John is referring to, we have to get alone with the One he had it with.

Motive and the Goal of Prayer

Many people pray for different reasons. Some of us pray because we learned that it's the right thing to do. Christians pray, so we should pray. Some of us pray because we have needs. Some of us pray because we are scared and freaked out. Some of us pray out of a sense of obligation and duty in order to prevent feelings of guilt over not "doing our devotions." Some of us pray in an effort to appear spiritual and draw attention to ourselves.

In Matthew 6, Jesus addresses something very important when it comes to prayer—motive. This is His commentary:

> When you pray, you are not to be like the hypocrites; for they love to stand and pray in the synagogues and on the street corners so that they may be seen by men. Truly I say to you, they have their reward in full. But you, when you pray, go into your inner room, close your door and pray to your Father who is in secret, and your Father who sees *what is done* in secret will reward you. And when you are praying, do not use meaningless repetition as the Gentiles do, for they suppose that they will be heard for their many words. So do not be like them; for your Father knows what you need before you ask Him.
>
> Matthew 6:5–8

Evidently, these Pharisees were a piece of work! But as easy as it might be to pick on them and point out the silliness of what they did in an effort to be noticed by people, we ought to take the log out of our own eye before pointing out the speck in theirs in an effort to make an example out of them. (See Matthew 7:3–5.)

The *why* behind our *what* is everything. Motive is so important and that's what Jesus is seeking to address in this passage. You can pray because you want people to view you as being "spiritual," or you can pray because you want to know Him. You do not have to use meaningless repetition of words. All you need to do is bring the sincerity of your heart. If you are sincere in your desire for intimacy with Him, you will find Him. He will reward you. But if you're goal is to be seen by men, you will have what you seek, but it will not be from the Lord.

You must be the steward of your own heart. You must know why it is that you are doing what you're doing. You have to be your own best friend. We can truly do so many things, even right and good things, from the wrong heart and a twisted motive. Take a look at these sobering words that Paul penned to the Corinthians:

> If I speak with the tongues of men and of angels, but do not have love, I have become a noisy gong or a clanging cymbal. If I have *the gift of* prophecy, and know all mysteries and all knowledge; and if I have all faith, so as to remove mountains, but do not have love, I am nothing. And if I give all my possessions to feed *the poor*, and if I surrender my body to be burned, but do not have love, it profits me nothing.
>
> 1 Corinthians 13:1–3

Paul is essentially saying this in regards to speaking with the tongues of men and of angels, having the gift of prophecy and faith, giving your possessions to feed the poor, and being martyred—these things are either done from the motive of love or the desire to make a name for yourself, be noticed by people, and draw attention to yourself. In other words, you can do all of these amazing spiritual realities and Godly principles and still make it all about *you*. Think about it. Giving your possessions to feed the poor is a good thing! It's a great thing! It's something God asks us to do! He asks us to take care of and feed the poor and yet Paul is saying you can do that, not have love as the motive, and walk away with nothing. Ah! That's crazy! He's even saying that you can surrender your body to be burned and the motive can *still* be selfish in nature while you breathe your last breath!

Take it a step further. You can prophecy, speak in tongues, have the gift of faith, perform miracles, and yet have Jesus say this to you:

> "Not everyone who says to Me, 'Lord, Lord,' will enter the kingdom of heaven, but he who does the will of My Father who is in heaven will enter. *Many will say to Me on that day, 'Lord, Lord, did we not prophesy in Your name, and in Your name cast out demons, and in Your name perform many miracles' "And then I will declare to them, 'I never knew you; depart from me, you who practice lawlessness'"* (emphasis mine).

Matthew 7:21–23

Why? It's *lawless* to do all of those things without the motive of love. It's lawless to prophesy, cast out demons, and perform miracles if it's all about the need to be loved and accepted and noticed by men. Jesus Himself said you could hang the whole law and the prophets on these two commandments—love God and your neighbor as yourself. (See Matthew 22:36–40.) If I do not have love, I have nothing. All I'll have is the reward I seek and if you're living out of the fear of man (the need to be esteemed and noticed by people) and not the fear of the Lord (the desire to be pleasing to Him, to revere Him, and to love the things He loves and hate the things He hates), you will have your reward. You'll be noticed by men. You may even be loved by them. But in the end, it will profit you nothing because selfishness is not from God. *Love is.* (See 1 John 4:7.)

Although I'm not an advocate of navel gazing (the art of constantly analyzing yourself to find out what's wrong with you), I do desire to have every false motive crushed within my life. I can promise you that I am not looking to do anything from selfishness or empty conceit. (See Philippians 2:3.) My heart's desire is for my life to be the embodiment of God's heart. I want all that I do to be from the motive of love that flows from a pure heart, good conscience, and a sincere faith. (See 1 Timothy 1:5.) That's why I'm not afraid to pray the same prayer David did in Psalm 139:23–24. "Search me, O God, and know my heart; Try me and know my anxious thoughts; And see if there be any hurtful way in me, And lead me in the everlasting way."

That prayer has to be one of the most honest prayers ever recorded. David is essentially saying, "I want to be just like you, God. I want to follow Your way. If there is anything within my heart, any false motive whatsoever, I want you to show it to me so that I can repent of it and move on and become what I desire."

If there is anything within my heart that even remotely looks like or smells like jealousy or selfish ambition, I want to know about it. I want to repent of it. I wasn't created to be jealous or to live selfishly. Life taught me that. If those things are in my heart, I want God to show them to me so I can see them for what they are, confess that it's not my desire to live that way, separate them from my identity in Christ, and pursue what it is that I really desire, which is to become just like my Father.

Despite the various reasons why people pray, very few people pray the way that Moses prayed.

"Then Moses said, 'I pray You, show me Your glory!'" (Exod. 33:18).

Moses was not asking God to show Him some mighty act or miracle. Moses had already seen the miracles God performed in Egypt. He saw the Red Sea part with his own eyes and felt the mist of the sea on his face as he passed through on dry ground. He heard the thunder, witnessed the flashes of lightning, and gazed upon the cloud that enveloped Mt. Sinai. When Moses prayed, "Show me Your glory," he was requesting to know God. He was asking God to reveal Himself to him. In Psalm 103:7, it says, "He made known His ways to Moses, His acts to the sons of Israel."

It would be feasible to say that Moses walked in understanding. He sought to know the counsel of the Lord. He wanted to know what made Him "tick." It wasn't enough to know the acts of God. He wanted to know His ways. He wanted to meet with Him.

Please don't get me wrong. It's okay to bring your supplications (needs) and requests to God in prayer. (See Philippians 4:6–7.) It's okay to cast your anxiety on Him because He cares for you. (See 1 Peter 5:7.) You're encouraged to do those things. But I believe we can walk with God in such a way that we understand He knows what we need before we ask Him. (See Matthew 6:8.) I believe we can truly seek His kingdom and His righteousness and know in our hearts that the things that concern us will be taken care of. (See Matthew 6:33.)

I believe it's time to go deeper in prayer. I believe that we must mature, guys. We can't simply seek God because of what He can do for us. We must seek *Him*. We must know *Him*. He is the goal of all prayer, Christ Himself. To *know* Him means to *become* like Him. Have you ever noticed how a couple who has been married for a long time can finish one another's sentences? My wife and I have been married for almost ten years. There have been numerous occasions as of late where I or she will say something and the other responds by saying, "I was thinking the same thing!" How does that happen? It happens because the two become one. It happens because there's an intimacy between the partners. It happens because two people deeply know one another, and when you know someone that deeply, *you can speak on their behalf and it would be as if they themselves were speaking*.

I want to become that close with God. Look at what Ephesians 5:31–32 says.

FOR THIS REASON A MAN SHALL LEAVE HIS FATHER AND MOTHER AND SHALL BE JOINED TO HIS WIFE, AND THE TWO SHALL BECOME ONE FLESH. This mystery is great; but I am speaking with reference to Christ and the church.

I want to experience with God what I am experiencing with my wife. It's what Paul refers to as a mystery, but it is profoundly beautiful. I want to finish His sentences. I want to be "one" with Him in a greater way and the only way I know how to do that is to seek Him.

Hebrews 11:6 tells us that the faith that pleases God is when we come to Him and *believe* that He is and that He is the rewarder of those who seek Him. The Greek word for *rewarder* is *misthapodotes*. It means one who pays wages. Remember the parable I referenced earlier about the man who hired out laborers to work in his vineyard? We can have what they had, guys.

To believe that "He is" is to believe that He is everything He says He is. He is I AM. To believe that "He is" is to believe that He exists. Why else would you pray if you didn't think He existed? And if He is rewarding those who *seek Him*, what is He rewarding you with? *Himself.* He's the goal of all prayer—*finding Him, knowing Him*—that's the name of the game. He is the reward.

> But whatever things were gain to me, those things I have counted as loss for the sake of Christ. More than that, I count all things to be loss in view of the surpassing value of knowing Christ Jesus my Lord, for whom I have suffered the loss of all things, and count them but rubbish so that I may gain Christ.
>
> Philippians 3:7–8

Climbing the Holy Mountain

In May of 2013, I believe I heard the Lord tell me to read 2 Peter 1. If you were to examine 2 Peter 1 in my Bible, you would notice that I've spent a significant amount of time studying and reading that chapter. Highlights, underlinings, and notes fill the page where that chapter resides. As I read through this chapter once more in faith believing that there was something God wanted to speak to me, I centered in on the following verses:

For we did not follow cleverly devised tales when we made known to you the power and coming of our Lord Jesus Christ, but we were eyewitnesses of His majesty. For when He received honor and glory from God the Father, such an utterance as this was made to Him by the Majestic Glory, "This is My beloved Son with whom I am well-pleased"— and we ourselves heard this utterance made from heaven when we were with Him on the holy mountain. *So* we have the prophetic word *made* more sure, to which you do well to pay attention as to a lamp shining in a dark place, until the day dawns and the morning star arises in your hearts.

2 Peter 1:16–19

Peter wrote these verses referring to the time that he, James, and John saw Jesus transfigured on a high mountain that Jesus Himself had led them up. (See Matthew 17:1–9, Mark 9:2–8, and Luke 9:28–36.) These three young men saw something that day that they had never seen before during their three-year tour of following Jesus on the earth. They saw the dead raised. They saw the sick healed. They saw demons cast out of people. They saw lepers cleansed. But despite all of these miraculous events, they did not contain within themselves what Peter says was revealed to himself and James and John on that day on the mountain with Jesus, His majesty.

The very eyes that saw lame men pick up their pallets and walk now saw what flesh had concealed for the last three years. Jesus was transformed right before their eyes. His appearance literally changed. His face shone as bright as the sun and His clothes became as white as light. Indeed, Peter, James, and John saw Jesus for who He really is, and it caused them to hit the deck! Despite their fear in that moment, they came to know Him in a greater way. They saw something that could not be revealed through the numerous people Jesus ministered to. They saw the *majesty* of the King. They saw the One who is described in the book of Revelation in this way:

Then I turned to see the voice that was speaking with me. And having turned I saw seven golden lampstands; and in the middle of the lampstands *I saw* one like a son of man, clothed in a robe reaching to the feet, and girded across His chest with a golden sash. His head and His hair were white like white wool, like snow; and His eyes were like a flame of fire. His feet *were* like burnished bronze, when it has been made to glow in a furnace, and His voice *was* like the sound of many waters. In His right hand He held seven stars, and out of His mouth came a sharp two-edged sword; and His face was like the sun shining in its strength.

Revelation 1:12–16

Now more than ever, I believe that Jesus is leading us up the holy mountain to be alone with Him so that He might reveal more of who He is to us. He is wanting us to have a greater revelation of His glory, holiness, and majesty. He wants us to know *Him.* The glory He was clothed in and revealed Himself in to Peter, James, and John is the glory He'll be returning in. It's His majesty that causes me to fear, but it's His goodness that causes me to not be afraid.

When I saw Him, I fell at His feet like a dead man. And He placed His right hand on me, saying, "Do not be afraid; I am the first and the last, and the living One; and I was dead, and behold, I am alive forevermore, and I have the keys of death and of Hades.

Revelation 1:17–18

He is God. And there is something greatly humbling about that. If He's God, that means we're not, and that's where the fear of the Lord begins. If He's God, He's to be revered. He's to be worshiped and adored. And despite all of this, He wants us to know Him intimately in the way He knows us. The King of kings wants to have a relationship with us. He wants us to climb the holy mountain.

The funny thing is that you do not climb this mountain with the strength of your grip, a harness, or climbing boots. You climb this mountain with your hands wide open, on your knees, and with humility.

"Who may ascend into the hill of the lord? And who may stand in His holy place? *He who has clean hands and a pure heart, Who has not lifted up his soul to falsehood And has not sworn deceitfully*" (Ps. 24:3–4; emphasis mine).

You cannot ascend the hill of the Lord if any of the following things are found within your heart:

> You lust and do not have; *so* you commit murder. You are envious and cannot obtain; *so* you fight and quarrel. You do not have because you do not ask. You ask and do not receive, because you ask with wrong motives, so that you may spend *it* on your pleasures.
>
> James 4:2–3

"But if you have bitter jealousy and selfish ambition in your heart, do not be arrogant and *so* lie against the truth" (Jas. 3:14).

James is not referring to the act of physical murder. He's referring to the murder that's committed within our hearts out of anger toward someone who is enjoying the benefit of something we don't have. It's anger driven by insecurity. Insecurity is the absence of security. People who are insecure do not know who they are so they desperately try to find themselves in all the wrong places. Insecurity causes a person to loathe and envy what someone else has believing that if they had it they'd feel important. Whenever we live that way, we are at the center of the universe. Living this way causes our hands to be stained with murder. You cannot ascend the hill of the Lord when your hands are unclean.

Unclean hands stained with murder causes a person to have an impure heart because they begin to ask for things out of envy and lust. They are driven by deficit (what they don't have) and insecurity begins to fuel their motive. They have no desire to love someone else. The only person they can think of is themselves because they are still trying to find who they are. If you're motive in seeking God is selfish in nature, you cannot ascend His mountain. We are not seeking Him to have a ministry, increase our platform and cause the spotlight to be tilted in our direction. If that is even remotely our motive, someone ought to tell us to chill and we ought to pull the plug on what we are doing.

The last thing that keeps you at the base of the mountain is when you lift up your soul to falsehood (exchange the truth for a lie) and swear deceitfully (live hypocritically). If you have selfish ambition and jealousy in your heart, deal with it. Acknowledge it. Don't lie against the truth and pretend to be something you're not. Get real. Don't live like a hypocrite. Don't put on a show for everyone else while masking what's really going on. Live with a good conscience, not a violated one. Be your own best friend. Know your heart. Confess what's going on, ask for forgiveness, and move on. Don't look back.

Listen to what Paul has to say concerning this matter in his letter to the Philippians:

> Brethren, I do not regard myself as having laid hold of *it* yet; but one thing *I do*: forgetting what *lies* behind and reaching forward to what *lies* ahead, I press on toward the goal for the prize of the upward call of God in Christ Jesus. Let us therefore, as many as are perfect, have this attitude; and if in anything you have a different attitude, God will reveal that also to you.
>
> Philippians 3:13–15

Nearly all of Philippians 3 deals with Paul's heartfelt desire to know Jesus. In the midst of his pursuit, he's purposed in his heart to not look back at the times he's missed it and fallen short. He keeps moving forward. He keeps looking ahead. You can't run a race looking backward. You run a race with your eyes fixed on the prize, the author and perfecter of your faith. (See Hebrews 12:1–2.)

The reality is I genuinely believe that if you are sincere within your own heart about wanting to know God, He will do in your life what Paul says above in verse 15. If you have a weird, twisted motive, God will reveal it to you. Why? Because you do desire to know Him and to not miss it. You don't wake up in the morning with a desire to live selfishly. You genuinely want to be just like your Father.

I truly believe that every person, for the most part, is fully aware of their motives. You ultimately know what drives you if you are honest with yourself. You know why you pray. You know why you do what you do. If you don't, you need to invite the Lord to search you and know your heart. There would have been a point in time where I would have been scared to do something like that. I would have been afraid of what He would find and what the repercussions might be. I would have been worried that He would be disappointed, but do you know what the funny thing is about all of those reasons? He already knows! He already knows what drives you and motivates you. He already knows what you are afraid He'll find! Asking Him to search you and know your heart is for your benefit. You can't repent of something you are ignorant of. You can invite Him to do it with confidence when you understand that He is good and that He is for you and that whatever He shows you, He shows you because He loves you. He wants to mature you. He wants to discipline you. That's what every good father does and it's the evidence that you are his son or daughter. He's producing the peaceful fruit of righteousness within us. (See Hebrews 12:5–11.)

We want the right heart behind all that we do and prayer is no different. We are not seeking to appear to be spiritual when we already are. You are in Him and He is in you. We are not seeking the approval of others when we already have His. We are not seeking to be noticed by men when His eye is already fixed on us. And we are not merely seeking Him because of what He can do for us. We want to become just like Him. We want to live what we claim we believe.

In the next two chapters, we will take a look at three postures of prayer that I believe will help all of us in the pursuit of knowing Him in a greater way and becoming what our hearts' desire. They are the answer to growing in the fellowship that the apostle John described and had with Jesus. Truly, prayer is where we seek God, fellowship with Him, commune with Him, and ask Him to open our eyes so that we might understand and truly believe what we claim we believe. There's no getting around it. You have to go to the source. We have to believe! We must grow in the reality of what the three women in the previous chapters experienced.

I will unpack two of the postures of prayer in the next chapter and the third in the chapter that follows.

The Secret Place

When *you* pray (emphasis mine).

—Matthew 6:6

It's Not as Difficult as It Sounds

Prayer is a funny thing. It's probably the one thing that all Christians know that they are supposed to do and yet so many do not know where to begin or how to get started. Even Jesus in the verse above assumes you are going to pray by saying, "When you pray," not, "*if* you pray." They hear other Christians discussing how they hear the voice of the Lord and describing the intimate times that they have with Jesus but are often left thinking, *Gee, that sounds wonderful, but I have no idea how to hear the voice of God or what it means to have intimacy with Jesus.* All too often, when people ask questions about how to hear the voice of God or what it means to cultivate a relationship with Him, many of us leaders and pastors and even other Christians have offered up these cheap words with no instruction or help. "Just go get alone with God." "You just have to pray." "Just be in His presence."

More than likely, we know what we mean when we say such things. For some of us, hearing the voice of God and growing in a relationship with Him is normal. It becomes second nature. But the truth is that many people have already tried our weak suggestions. They've heeded our words out of the respect they have for us but when they get alone with God the only thing they can think of is, *Okay. I'm alone. Now what?* As a result, many Christians treat prayer like a thirty-day, money-back guarantee. "Try it. See if you like it. If you don't, you can always send it back, and we will refund your money to you." They've given up because it seems like it doesn't work. They may even think that they are doing something wrong.

My goal in the next two chapters is to equip you in the three veins of prayer I often flow in and out of. The truth is that you can flow in and out of all three of these postures at the same time. Although their functions appear different, they can ultimately yield the same result. Again, the goal of all prayer is Christ Himself. It's the desire to know Him and become like Him in every way. We want to receive as the outcome of our faith, the salvation of our souls. (See 1 Peter 1:9.) In other words, we want to think and feel like heaven and align our will with it as well.

First and foremost, it is my conviction that in order to pray effectively and begin a lifestyle of prayer, you must begin with and understand and possess these three simple things (these are not in any particular order)—belief, desire, alone.

You have to believe that you can hear the voice of God. In John 10:27, Jesus says that His sheep *hear* His voice. That's us, guys. We either believe that or we don't. It doesn't matter what your experiences have been like in the past when it has come to prayer. The Bible says that you can hear His voice. This is foundational in our pursuit of Him. This must be a reality if we are to pray. Conversations are not one-way streets. When we pray, we are not simply doing all the talking. God has things He wants to tell you. Everything He wants to say to us is accomplished through the role of the Holy Spirit in our lives. It's the Holy Spirit who teaches us all things and brings to remembrance all that Jesus has spoken to us. (See John 14:26.) Have you ever been in a situation where you needed encouragement and a specific verse came to your mind? That's the Holy Spirit reminding you of all that Jesus has spoken to you. Have you ever needed wisdom and guidance in an area of your life and suddenly you received the "know-how" and insight needed to make a certain decision? Have you ever been able to do something that you were never able to do before? That's the Holy Spirit teaching you all things.

The Holy Spirit also reveals Jesus to you and causes you to grow in understanding. (See John 15:26.) He's the One who is the Spirit of truth and who guides us into all truth. (See John 16:13.) Have you ever had an experience where you are reading scripture and suddenly you see something you never saw before and it causes something within you to come alive in a greater way that causes you to feel like you were being born again, again? That's the Holy Spirit revealing Jesus to you and growing you in understanding. He's the One who causes the light to come on in a greater way. He's the giver of revelation.

The Holy Spirit will also disclose to you what is to come. (See John 16:13.) This is the heartbeat and essence of prophecy. The Holy Spirit is the dispenser of spiritual gifts. (See 1 Corinthians 12:11.) Prophecy is one of those gifts, and it operates out of His *knowing*, not our understanding. He's the One who knows what is to come and He reveals it to who He wills or so desires. In the introduction of this book, I wrote about how I kept seeing the number 11 everywhere. Through witnessing the reoccurrence of that number, I believe the Holy Spirit revealed to me what is coming upon the body of Christ at large—*a great awakening*. He spoke to me prophetically.

Please keep in mind that this book has not been written to help you recognize the different ways that God speaks to people. There are plenty of other great books that have been written to equip you and help you in that area. The point I'm trying to make through these examples is God speaks and you can hear His voice, but it begins with you believing that you can.

It also begins with desire. You have to desire to know Him. You have to desire to hear His voice. If you don't, your efforts will quickly turn into works. You'll pray because you're supposed to and because it's the right thing to do. But if you are sincere and you genuinely desire Him, prayer becomes effortless. It's a joy to find the object of your desire. It's a joy to be alone with the One who desires you.

"I am my beloved's, And his desire is for me" (Song 7:10).

Shortly after my second daughter, Lily, was born, my wife's grandmother, Nana, had come to stay with us to help us with the transition of growing from one child to having two children. She arrived the day of my wife's scheduled C-section to care for and watch our oldest daughter, Emma, while I spent time in the hospital with my wife and newborn. At night, I would venture home to sleep and to give Emma the comfort and security that comes from knowing that Daddy is home. My presence was the calm to her uncertainty and sudden change in our family.

Nana and I would often stay up late talking into the night. One evening, she said, "I read your book, you know [*First Dance: Venturing Deeper into a Relationship with God*]. In it, you talk about how you can just pray for hours and hours. I've been a Christian nearly all my life and I don't understand that. How do you do that? How did you get to that place?"

Her question was so sincere. She genuinely wanted to know how I was able to have such a desire. Because I wasn't prepared for her question, I gave a generic response. Truthfully, I no longer remember what it was that I had said to her. I just know the answer wasn't sufficient. It didn't "feel" right. But I did the best I could in trying to explain my hunger to her.

After our conversation had ended, I made my way up to bed. While praying in my room, I heard God ask me, "Brian, do you know what the strength of your prayer life is?"

"No," I responded.

Even though I didn't know the answer, I knew I was about to find out what the answer was. I thought it was pretty cool that it was as if God and I were continuing the conversation that Nana and I were having moments earlier. It was as if He was asking me the same question that Nana was seeking an answer to, only this time He was going to answer the question for me.

In regards to the strength of my prayer life, he said, "You settled in your heart a long time ago that I desire you."

What God was saying was, "Your desire for Me was born when you discovered how much I desire you." It's true. I want to chase the One who has chased me from day one. I love because He first loved me. (See 1 John 4:19.)

The beautiful thing about desire is that if you lack it, you can pray for it. It's integral to confess something to God such as "Lord, I know that I should probably have a greater desire to seek you and to know you, but I don't. Would you help me to desire you? Would you cause a fire to burn within me that can only be stoked and fanned through spending time with you? And could you teach me how to pray and what it means to have fellowship with you? I know it's your desire to have a relationship with me. I want to have one with you too. Come father me in this area. In Jesus's name. Amen."

Believing that you can hear His voice teamed up with a desire to know Him will result in you setting aside the time to get alone to hear His voice and seek Him. It's the only way. The best thing to do when cultivating a relationship with God is to turn off all the noise, unplug, get rid of all the distractions and get alone with Him. If you want to get to know someone, you have to spend time with them. If you want His voice to be louder in your life, you have to silence everything else around you.

"But you, when you pray, go into your inner room, close your door and pray to your Father who is in secret, and your Father who sees *what is done* in secret will reward you" (Matt. 6:6).

Leonard Ravenhill makes the following statements concerning the discipline of praying in secret in an article[1] that he had written on prayer:

> God makes all His best people in loneliness. Do you know what the secret of praying is? Praying in secret. *"But you, when you pray, go into your inner room, and when you have shut your door..." (Matt. 6:6).* You can't show off when the

door's shut and nobody's there. You can't display your gifts. You can impress others, but you can't impress God.

Throughout the ages, God has seemingly made Himself known to those in secret. He made Himself known to Moses at the burning bush (see Exodus 3:2)—*alone.* He made Himself known to Samuel who was lying down in the temple before the ark (see 1 Samuel 3:2–4)—*alone.* He made Himself known to Elijah on a mountain through a gentle blowing (see 1 Kings 19:11–13)—*alone.* And He wants to make Himself known to you—*alone.* He's personal. He's relational. Praying in secret is the place where intimacy occurs. It's just you and Him. No one else is watching. You seek Him. You wait for Him. You talk to Him and share your heart with Him. You listen for Him and He shares His heart with you. When you do this, you are either crazy and talking to absolutely no one or God is real and He hears you. I'm banking on not being crazy. My chips are all in on the fact that He hears me and that He rewards those who seek Him.

Now that we have covered what I believe is a healthy foundation for a life of prayer, I'd now like to introduce you to three ways you can put belief, desire, and being alone with God into practice. Please understand that these three methods are by no means exhaustive. They are the three ways I am most familiar and comfortable with.

Watch and Pray

I know that what I am about to write in this section will run the risk of possibly sounding legalistic to some. That is certainly not my intention. The goal behind writing this portion of the book is to help people to understand what Leonard Ravenhill meant when he would say things such as *"You are as spiritual as you want to be."* You can't be rich in one thing without being poor in another. You're either rich in the things of God and poor in the things of self or rich in self and poor in the things of God.

Remember, it's over the joy of what we found that we sell all that we have in order to obtain the wealth of what we discovered. (See Matthew 13:44.) The truth, guys, is that we find what we seek. We have what we asked for. And what's been opened is because we've knocked. As much as God loves to chase after us and woo us; He likes to be chased after and wooed as well.

There was a season in my life when I was waking up at 4:00 a.m. to do the very thing I'm about to share with you. I did it out of hunger. I did it because I believed He wanted me to do it and God's grace was upon it. I have found that whenever I try to implement a discipline without the grace of God, it becomes tedious and difficult. To be honest with you, it's straight up annoying! And it quickly turns into works. Although I've been walking with God for fifteen years up to this point, I'm starting to understand what Jesus meant when He said, "Apart from Me you can do nothing" (John 15:5). I need His grace upon all that I do; otherwise, I find myself living out of my own strength.

During this time of waking up at 4:00 a.m., God taught me something significant about prayer. He used these three simple words to reveal to me a very profound lesson—*watch and pray*. These three words can be found tucked away in a passage of scripture found in Matthew 26:36–41. It's here that we read about how Jesus spent His few remaining hours of earthly life before His crucifixion. This is how Matthew records it.

> Then Jesus came with them to a place called Gethsemane, and said to His disciples, "Sit here while I go over there and pray." And He took with Him Peter and the two sons of Zebedee, and began to be grieved and distressed. Then He said to them, "My soul is deeply grieved, to the point of death; remain here and keep watch with Me." And He went a little beyond *them*, and fell on His face and prayed, saying, "My Father, if it is possible, let this cup pass from Me; yet not as I will, but as You will." And He came to the disciples and found them sleeping, and said to Peter, "*So,*

you men could not keep watch with Me for one hour? Keep watching and praying that you may not enter into temptation; the spirit is willing, but the flesh is weak" (emphasis mine).

Matthew 26:36–41

It is my belief that Jesus's instructions had nothing to do with watching and praying so that Peter, James, and John would not enter into the temptation of scattering. He told them in verse 31 of the same chapter that they would all fall away because of Him. If Jesus said it, it's going to happen. There is no arguing with the red-letters. The sheep scatter when the shepherd is struck down. He's not telling them to be on guard against something that has already been prophesied and will come to pass. He's teaching them a principle in His darkest hour. He's cautioning them to be aware of the temptation of *not praying*. Why? Because the spirit is willing but the flesh is weak.

The last thing your flesh wants to do is pray. There are countless other ways that your flesh would love to spend its time. The flesh craves carnal pleasure. It's gluttonous in nature. It prefers abundance and despises balance. It'd rather be out of control than disciplined. It wants to be the center of attention. It wants to be satisfied and hates being crucified. It wants to sleep, eat, and be entertained. Your spirit, however, longs to commune with God. Its interest is in the will of God and to be pleasing to Him. One of the ways you kill the voice of the flesh and feed the hunger of your spirit is to watch and pray.

The first thing I'd like to point out is that *"watching* and *praying"* is the catalyst that leads us to the words of Peter and John "For we cannot stop speaking about what we have *seen* and *heard"* (Acts 4:20). Watching has to do with seeing. Praying has to do with listening. Let me explain.

Watching and praying leads to a life of great expectation and anticipation. To watch and pray implies that you are waiting on the Lord and listening. You're waiting for Him to move, to answer prayer, to show you things, to reveal Himself in a greater way, and to speak. The reason you are watching is because you believe. You have faith for God to do the thing you are waiting for. You expect. You anticipate all because you have a hope that's an anchor to your soul. (See Hebrews 6:19.) Your hope is in Him and His ability to perform. Even though I have quoted this verse in other places throughout this book, I will quote it again: He who promised is faithful. (See Hebrews 10:23.) To watch is to wait upon His ability to be faithful to what it is that He has promised. Even though you may not be speaking to God, watching is prayer. Watching contains words when no utterance is found within your mouth. It's faith. It's believing that He is the rewarder of those who seek Him.

A great example of this is evidenced through the testimony of the minivan that was given to my wife and I that I referenced earlier in the book. I believed with all my heart that God knew what I needed before I asked. He was well aware that my family was growing. He was not taken aback by the fact that I needed a vehicle that could seat six people. As a result, I *watched* for that van. I waited for it. I knew it was coming. It was only a matter of time. I often considered His faithfulness and ability to carry out His promises while praying.

You can watch and pray with your eyes open. You can watch and pray with your eyes closed. But you should do it in silence. Be free of distractions. Give yourself every opportunity to hear the faintest whisper and to see the clearest of visions.

You watch and pray because you are convinced. You wait because you have an answer. And it doesn't matter how long it takes because the only thing that counts is the word of God.

Indeed, to watch and pray requires an act of our will. By choosing to pray, we are in essence telling God the very thing Jesus did. "Not my will, but yours be done." Alas, here lies the difference between Adam and Jesus. In the first garden (Eden), man's will was done. In the second garden (Gethsemane), man's will was surrendered. The battle that was lost in the first garden was won in the second. While praying in the garden of Gethsemane, Jesus was communing with His Father. He was speaking, saying, "My Father, if this [the suffering Jesus was about to endure] cannot pass away unless I drink it, Your will be done" (Matt. 26:42). He vocalized the grief and distress that was within His own heart. And He waited. He listened. He watched to see if His Father would show Him another way. He *watched* for the answer to His *prayer*. Even when His soul had become deeply grieved to the point of death (see Matthew 26:38) and His flesh didn't want to be torn, Jesus still watched. Jesus still prayed.

By choosing to watch and pray, we are also accomplishing and experiencing the following things:

- Watching and praying keeps us sober and vigilant. It increases discernment and recognizes the snare of the temptation to not pray and seek God.
- Watching and praying sharpens your ability to hear the voice of God.
- Watching and praying joins the Lord in intercession and causes us to be ready to pray whatever it is that He may tell you to pray.
- Watching and praying causes you to rise up with wings like eagles, to run and not get tired, and to walk and not grow weary (Isa. 40:31).
- Watching and praying is being still and knowing that He's God (Ps. 46:10).
- Watching and praying increases faith.

It was through these three words that I began to expect and anticipate that God would reveal Himself to me in a greater way. I would literally get alone and sit in silence and wait for God to show me things or tell me things. There's something about getting up early in the morning when it's still dark outside and no one else is awake. It's quiet. That's when you know this is for real and you aren't playing games. Although I haven't roused myself out of bed at 4:00 a.m. for quite some time as a result of the twins being born, I still find the time to seek Him. In fact, I'm aware that most people do not feel like they have the time to seek God in the capacity they'd like because of the responsibilities they have. Let's face it, some of us are fathers and mothers. Some of us have to go to work and go to school. But whatever the responsibility is, do not allow it to become an excuse that robs you of taking advantage of any moment of time you may have.

Watch and pray in the shower. Watch and pray in the car. Watch and pray while feeding a baby. Watch and pray when the kids are asleep. Watch and pray early in the morning before the sun even has a chance to awaken. You can find the time. You can do this. Over time, you will find yourself heeding Paul's exhortation to pray without ceasing. (See 1 Thessalonians 5:17.) Before you know it, you will begin to live with a consciousness of God. You may not be seeking Him with the door closed, but you are seeking Him and watching and praying in your continual thoughts about Him. You learn to set your mind on things above and to dwell on beautiful and lovely things. (See Colossians 3:2 and Philippians 4:8.)

Meditation

Meditation and watching and praying go hand in hand. They are both acts of faith. Both can be practiced at the same time without even realizing it. While watching and praying, you are essentially meditating on the faithfulness of God. While meditating, you are watching what you are meditating on through prayer become a reality. You meditate on what it is you are waiting for. You're conscious of it. It's in the forefront of your mind. As a result, faith rises. The more you meditate on His faithfulness, the greater the faith you have in His ability to carry out His "yes" toward you. (See 2 Corinthians 1:20.)

Meditation is the place where feelings are pushed aside and truth is elevated. It's here where you begin to learn to live by faith and not by your emotions. Truth becomes your teacher, not the instability of feelings that often follow the changes of circumstances or opinions of people. You muse, ponder, and think about whatever promise or truth has gripped your heart and attention. It's the place where you become rooted and grounded in belief. Your mind begins to be renewed. You fill your soul with God's reality, which thereby displaces the lies we've been fed most of our lives by life itself. As a result, your eye begins to change. You see things according to the truth that's growing inside of you.

Indeed, meditation is the one mode of prayer that has helped me in so many ways. It causes His word to come alive in me. I've also found that the more I meditate on something the bigger it gets. Revelation is a byproduct of meditation. The more you mediate on a specific verse or idea, the more God speaks to you through it.

Let's look at Psalm 1:1–3 together to better understand the benefits of meditation and what it is.

> How blessed is the man who does not walk in the counsel of the wicked, Nor stand in the path of sinners, Nor sit in the seat of scoffers! But his delight is in the law of the LORD, And in His law he meditates day and night. He will be like a tree *firmly* planted by streams of water, Which yields its fruit in its season And its leaf does not wither; And in whatever he does, he prospers.

The word *meditates* in this passage is translated from the Hebrew word *hagah*. It means "to moan or groan, growl, utter, speak, muse." Moaning, groaning, and growling are inarticulate sounds. They are often present when someone is in pain emotionally or physically. They can be found when someone is frustrated or disappointed. But they can also be present as a result of God doing a deep work within a person's heart. Hebrews 4:12 sheds light on this process by saying, "For the word of God is living and active and sharper than any two-edged sword, and piercing as far as the division of soul and spirit, of both joints and marrow, and able to judge the thoughts and intentions of the heart" (Heb. 4:12).

Indeed, the word of God is a scalpel in the hands of the Holy Spirit. The word of God always gets to the "heart" of the matter. It trims the fat and removes the deadweight of the lies we've believed. Because meditation is very much the same as abiding, the word of the Lord through meditation prunes us so that we may bear more fruit. (See John 15:2.) The word of God also exposes our motives. It reveals the thoughts and intentions of our hearts. It brings light to the darkness.

Truly, the word does many things. It matures us. It feeds us. It heals us. It transforms us. And yet in the process of these many wonderful things, we sometimes find ourselves moaning, groaning, and maybe even growling through the transformation that takes place through meditating on the word of God. Why? Because old ways of thinking and believing are dying and new ones are being formed. Sometimes, our old ways kick and scream on their way out causing us to moan or growl through the labor pains of being transformed.

As I already mentioned above, the word *meditate* also means "to utter, speak, or muse." Whereas *moaning, groaning*, and *growling* are incoherent sounds without form, uttering, speaking, or musing are the exact opposites. When meditating on the word, you may whisper, murmur, or say aloud a word or verse you've just read. You can also do this in silence. You do not have to make sounds with your mouth in order to utter or speak. You can do it in your own mind, which is the practice I am most comfortable with. I often find myself pondering a verse or thinking about God in some way in the quiet of my own soul. In fact, I spent nearly a year or more meditating on the fact that He loved me until it became a greater reality in my life. The crazy thing is that there's still more to meditate on when it comes to His love! There's even more room for me to grow in understanding its height, length, breadth, and depth, but meditation is the key as I watch and pray for it to get bigger still.

Getting back to Psalm 1:1–3, let's begin to look at this passage verse by verse in order to further develop and equip you in the practice of meditation.

"How blessed is the man who does not walk in the counsel of the wicked, Nor stand in the path of sinners, Nor sit in the seat of scoffers!" (Ps. 1:1).

When I read a verse like this one above and see that I can be blessed by living out what it is that produces the blessing, I want to put whatever those things may be into action! It is truly not my desire to receive advice from the wicked or practice sin or keep bad company that corrupts good morals (see 1 Corinthians 15:33) or sit down where the mockers gather. Because I'm not a partaker in these realities, I'm a blessed man! The Bible tells me so! But the reason I don't partner with such habits is because my heart has been transformed through the blood of Christ. I've been born again, and as a result, my desires have changed. Indeed, the blood of Christ made the practices in verse one null and void in my life and gave birth to verse two within me.

"But his delight is in the law of the LORD, And in His law he meditates day and night" (Ps. 1:2).

Without becoming overly technical, it's sufficient to say that we can substitute the word *law* in this verse with the word *word* and still do this verse justice and maintain its integrity. Truthfully, the art of meditation (if I can say it that way) is nothing new to any of us. Your mind is always dwelling on something albeit it good or bad. So many of us, unfortunately, have meditated on the wrong things for far too long. It's the meditation of thoughts that leads to beliefs. Wrong thinking will inevitably lead to wrong believing. Because I thought wrongly about myself for so long based on how I was treated and the things that were said about me, I believed wrongly about me. Meditating on the truth of God's word begins to turn the cruise ship of wrong thinking and believing in a brand new direction.

Because so many of us are unable to read the Bible day and night as this verse would seemingly suggest due to having to raise children, drive to work, clean the house, etc., there must be another way to do this, right? *Right.* There is another way. What I'm about to do now is show you how this concept plays out in my own prayer life. Honestly, you can do this anytime, anywhere through the still, small voice in your mind or out loud. I will list different ideas/realities and show you what it looks like for me to meditate on these things through prayer. As you read, you will take notice of various verses that are laced throughout these prayers. Although I do not quote the verses verbatim nor mention the book and chapter where they are found, they grow and grow in richness and in depth throughout the particular prayers. They become more real. As you pray them and think upon them, their truths become larger within your own heart.

These are prayers of affirmation through faith and relationship. What I mean by that is this: when I meditate, I am affirming what I know to be truth through the word of God and talk to Him about it relationally. These are not "confessions." This is me talking to my Father. It's relational. Please keep in mind that I am not writing these prayers so that you might make them your own and pray them verbatim. In fact, I'm praying as I write them and I'm shortening them for the sake of space. I'm merely showing you examples of things I affirm to myself and think upon. Because prayer is personal, it will look different for you.

God's Love:

> Father, I thank you that you love me. I know that you love me because you sent Your Son. No one pays a high price for nothing and you paid the highest price for me. You wanted me when I didn't want myself. You loved me when I didn't love myself. Even when I wanted nothing to do with You, Your heart never changed toward me. I'm so thankful that You came to find me. You laid Your life down for me and now nothing can separate me from Your love. You didn't come to judge me. You came to save me.

And it's your great love that has caused me to become your son. Thank you for fathering me. Thank you for disciplining me. Thank you that Your love for me kills the voice of fear in my life. Thank you that Your love caused me to come alive.

My Identity in Christ:

Father, I thank you that I am a new creation. I thank you that the old is gone and the new has come. My heart has absolutely no agreement with sin. I've been made brand new. You have made me righteous. I stand squeaky clean before you. My standing had nothing to do with what I did. It's because of what You have done. I can approach your throne with confidence and boldness because I stand holy before you in Your sight. You've made me Your son, and I desire to please you. All that You are has come to make its home in me. I am learning to think and feel just like You. Your ways are becoming my ways and as You are so am I in this world. You became what I was so I could become what You are. I stand before You just as if I had never sinned. I was dead and you made me alive. You have caused me to be born again. You are my Father. I have a brand-new Dad.

Answered Prayer:

Father, I thank you that You are faithful. I thank you that I can put my trust in you. Every answered prayer reaffirms these realities. You really do care about me. You really do know what I need before I ask you. I thank you that every good and perfect gift comes from You. I know that whatever I ask in Your name that's in accordance with Your will, you hear and answer me. Thank you for your blessings in my life. Thank you for loving me and for showing Yourself strong. Thank you for being a father to me. Thank you for this testimony.

I'll now take some verses that I have referenced different times throughout this book to illustrate what it looks like to meditate upon scripture itself.

"For the Son of Man has come to seek and to save that which was lost" (Luke 19:10).

> Father, I thank you that you sent Your Son to find me and to save me. I was lost. I did not know the way home. But you loved me enough to show me. You loved me enough to pull me out of death and into life. I believed so wrongly about myself for so long, but you showed me the truth. I hid behind addictions and nearly killed myself through them, and yet you extended Your hand to me. You loved the very thing I was destroying. You never gave up on me even though I gave up on myself. You stepped in at the right time. You can fly faster than I can fall. You saved my life not only spiritually, but physically as well. You have put an end to every addiction in my life. You found me and You are never letting go.

"For your Father knows what you need before you ask Him" (Matt. 6:8).

> Father, I'm so thankful that I can trust you. I'm thankful that you know what I need and when I need it. You are so good. Your timing is always perfect. You are always faithful. There has never been a time when you weren't good. There's never been a time when you weren't faithful. It's who You are. Everything you do flows from Your being. You've always taken care of me. I'm thankful that whatever concerns me is taken care of because I seek You and Your kingdom. You are the provider of every good and perfect gift. I'm more valuable to You than many birds. You know everything about me. You're my Father and I give myself to You and Your ability to keep me.

"God, after He spoke long ago to the fathers in the prophets in many portions and in many ways, in these last days has spoken to us in His Son, whom He appointed heir of all things, through whom also He made the world" (Heb. 1:1–2).

> First and foremost, Father, I'm thankful that you want me to know You. You want me to discover the deepest things about You. It's Your good pleasure to share Yourself with me and to tell me things about Yourself. You love me enough to speak to me and You have revealed Yourself to the world through Your Son. We can all know you now. You are not hiding. You caused Your very word to become flesh. It was Your idea to become like us so that we might know You. There's nothing you want more than for me to grow in relationship with You. You want to talk to me. You want to walk with me. I can hear Your voice. I'm thankful that you teach me and train me. I'm thankful that eternal life is knowing You, Father, and Jesus Christ whom You sent. I'm thankful, Holy Spirit, that you reveal Jesus to me and bring all things that He has spoken to my remembrance. Thanks for leading me into the truth.

Meditation is certainly one of the ways where the things you've read up to this point become a reality in your own life. Meditation is where you take the stories of the woman with the alabaster vial, the woman at the well, and the woman caught in adultery and ponder and think upon them until something is stirred up within you. You practice this discipline so that the Gospel comes alive inside of you and the beauty of what Jesus did is all you can see and live. Remember, true believing is evidenced through the life we live, not the words we say. Talk is cheap. People want to *see* our lives, not hear our opinions. We practice watching and praying and meditation because we want to live this thing. We want to become what He is toward us. We want to honor the fact that all of creation is waiting for us to get this. (See Romans 8:19.)

Because we are building a history with God, it's important to also meditate on all that He has done for you. Every testimony of what God has done in your life is a building block in the foundation of your relationship with Him that prepares you for the next trial in your life. Remembrance is what causes you to pass every test. When you *know* the material, there isn't a single exam you can't ace. Because my wife and I will always be able to recall the fact that God gave us a minivan, we will be better equipped to trust Him in greater circumstances. Be at all times ready to recall what the Lord has done. Give thanks to His name.

The Outcome of Meditation

Now that we discussed the practice of meditating on the word, let's take a look at the rest of Psalm 1:1–3 and see what the byproduct is.

"He will be like a tree *firmly* planted by streams of water, Which yields its fruit in its season And its leaf does not wither; And in whatever he does, he prospers" (Ps 1:3).

Did you see that? *He will be.* It's a promise, guys. God promises that you will be rooted and grounded. You will have the necessary fruit in every situation. And you will prosper in all that you do. Why? Because you are learning to think and act like heaven. Everything you hear, see, and go through must be filtered through what you believe, and as your mind becomes filled and transformed by the word of God, you will respond to all that life throws at you according to the word of God. You won't be tossed to and fro by the storms of life. You'll be firmly planted.

In this next and last chapter, we will take a look at the last posture of prayer—desperation. Indeed, this is the posture that I found myself in for nearly all of 2013 and continue to find myself in. But as I said before, watching and praying, meditation, and desperation flow in and out of one another. All three can be utilized and practiced at one time. I'll do my best to explain this phenomenon in the coming pages.

Desperation

"She, greatly distressed, prayed to the LORD and wept bitterly."

—1 Samuel 1:10

The Cry of My Heart

I am going to be brutally honest in this chapter. Don't get me wrong. It's not that I haven't been honest with you up until this point of the book. I have been. It's just that I am going to bear my own heart before you. I want to be transparent with you because I believe that authenticity is extremely important in our relationships with God and one another. But I also believe that my openness will help to tie all the loose ends of this book together. Indeed, this book is a mirror of my own life. I can only write out of what I understand or am currently walking through. I have often found that the things that God has had me preach are first and foremost for me.

When God spoke the words "no more games" to me at the beginning of 2013, He didn't do it so I could create a sermon series out of them. No. Those words were just as much for me, if not more, as they were for the ones I'd be sharing them with.

When God had me hone in on the woman with the alabaster vial, the woman at the well, and the woman caught in adultery, He didn't do it so that I could write a book about those three women one day. He did it because He wants the beauty of what they found and experienced to become a greater reality within my own life.

When God continuously highlighted the number 11 to me, He didn't do it so I could share about it in all of the different prophetic circles. He did it because He was showing me that it's time that I wake up as much as everyone else. We're a family. What's true for you is true for me.

Frankly, I'm tired of not taking the Gospel as serious as I'd like to. If this thing (the Gospel) is really real, it should *consume* us—literally. We should be overtaken by it. We should be smitten with it. I'm ashamed that at times I claim with my mouth that I'm hungry for God only to spend countless hours entertaining myself with social media or television. I'm tired of claiming I believe something that I am unwilling to live out because of fear. I hate the fact that the possibility of rejection is still a blip on my radar. I'm tired of being frustrated toward circumstances and people. I hate that hiccups of the old me pop up from time to time. And I wish I wouldn't get frustrated toward my own children when they don't listen.

I want to cry tears for the lost. I want a revelation of eternity. I want to live my life for the Day of Judgment. And I want integrity in every area of my life. What I mean by that is I don't want to merely have an opinion and know the right answers. I want to become my opinion and be the right answers. I want to live my life fully awake. I want to believe. I want to be fully convinced and fully persuaded. I must become like Him in every way. I want to think the way He thinks. I want to feel what He feels. And I want to say what He would say.

Actually, there's integrity within the act of confession. When James tells us to confess our sins to one another (see James 5:16), I believe he is referring to the very thing I'm trying to do here. Why? Because James also explains that to those of us who know the right thing to do and don't do it, to us it is a sin. (See James 4:17.) Let's get real. We know the right thing to do, but how many of us are doing it? Many of us have been educated past our level of obedience. Many of us could teach on healing and how to pray for the sick, prophecy, evangelism, etc., but that doesn't mean we are living those things! Jesus said that wisdom was vindicated by her deeds (see Matthew 11:19), not by her opinions! In other words, the proof is in the pudding. It's in the doing.

Some of you might say, "Calm down, buddy. Take it easy!" Trust me, the last thing I need to do is calm down and take it easy. I do not think that when I stand before the judgment seat of Christ that Jesus is going to accuse me of taking Him too seriously! Jonathan Edwards, the man that God had used to usher in the first Great Awakening and who preached the famous sermon "Sinners in the Hands of an Angry God," was quoted as saying, "Lord, stamp eternity on my eyeballs." I believe we would be a completely different breed of people if we understood the fact that we will all stand before Him one day. (See Romans 14:10.)

I need God to become more real in my life! I need His forgiveness, His love, His mercy, and His power to possess me! I'm desperate. It's getting to the point where I tell Him things such as "Unless You do a deeper work in my heart, just pull the plug now. I don't want to do this anymore." I need Him to help me believe. If we aren't living it, we aren't believing it. I'm tired of saying I believe in healing only to walk past person after person. I hate that I claim I believe in hell only to pass by one person after the other without so much as a thought of where they might spend eternity. That's not okay with me and it shouldn't be okay with anyone else that has a belief they do not exercise.

To put it plainly, I'm frustrated. That's the only way I can explain it. I'm tired of being where I am. I want the incongruence between the confession of my mouth and the life that I live done away with. And the only way I know how to deal with the things I've mentioned is to take them to the One that knows what to do with them in prayer.

The Source

The desperation I am experiencing is the result of the desires of my heart. I desire to be a godly father and husband. I desire to love people with *all* that I am. I desire to share the gospel and pray for every sick person I see. I desire to take the gospel seriously and become like Jesus. I desire to be overtaken by love. I desire to know Him more. I desire to live integral and without hypocrisy. I desire to act upon what I claim I believe. I desire these things because they are the very things that God wants in my own life. Desire comes from Him. It's born out of a relationship with Him. Intimacy results in conception. Desire is the seed of God planted within your heart.

I mentioned this idea earlier in chapter 4 when I shared about Hannah and Shiloh. Truthfully, there was no one more desperate than Hannah in the entire Bible. The only person who might come close is Rachel who became jealous of her sister, Leah, and said to Jacob, "Give me children, or else I die." (See Genesis 30:1.) That's some desperation. That's a petition. I wonder if any of us would ever desire to get to that place in our relationship with God where we so desire to know Him in such a way that if He doesn't reveal more of who He is, we would rather die. I believe the body of Christ is heading in that direction. They are tired of not seeing and not hearing. Such hunger is a sign that we are awake. Being desperate and hungry for God reveals that we aren't sleeping. We care. We are vigilant. We are watching and praying.

Hannah's Story

Although we took a brief look at Hannah's story before, we will explore it again in more detail. Because we will reference her story throughout this chapter, I thought it would be a good idea to include it in its entirety. Here it is for your reading pleasure:

Now there was a certain man from Ramathaim-zophim from the hill country of Ephraim, and his name was Elkanah the son of Jeroham, the son of Elihu, the son of Tohu, the son of Zuph, an Ephraimite. He had two wives: the name of one was Hannah and the name of the other Peninnah; and Peninnah had children, but Hannah had no children. Now this man would go up from his city yearly to worship and to sacrifice to the LORD of hosts in Shiloh. And the two sons of Eli, Hophni and Phinehas, were priests to the LORD there. When the day came that Elkanah sacrificed, he would give portions to Peninnah his wife and to all her sons and her daughters; but to Hannah he would give a double portion, for he loved Hannah, but the LORD had closed her womb. Her rival, however, would provoke her bitterly to irritate her, because the LORD had closed her womb. It happened year after year, as often as she went up to the house of the LORD, she would provoke her; so she wept and would not eat. Then Elkanah her husband said to her, "Hannah, why do you weep and why do you not eat and why is your heart sad? Am I not better to you than ten sons?" Then Hannah rose after eating and drinking in Shiloh. Now Eli the priest was sitting on the seat by the doorpost of the temple of the LORD. She, greatly distressed, prayed to the LORD and wept bitterly. She made a vow and said, "O LORD of hosts, if You will indeed look on the affliction of Your maidservant and remember me, and not forget Your maidservant, but will give Your maidservant a son, then I will give him to the LORD all the days of his life, and a razor shall never come on his head." Now it came about, as she continued praying before the LORD, that Eli was watching her mouth. As for Hannah, she was speaking in her heart, only her lips were moving, but her voice was not heard. So Eli thought she was drunk. Then Eli said to her, "How long will you make yourself drunk? Put away your wine from you." But Hannah replied, "No, my lord, I am a woman oppressed in spirit; I have drunk neither wine nor strong drink, but I have poured out my soul before the LORD. "Do not consider your maidservant as a worthless woman, for I have spoken until now out of my great concern and provocation." Then Eli answered and said, "Go in peace; and may the God of Israel grant your petition that you have asked of Him." She said, "Let your maidservant find favor in your sight." So the woman went her way and ate, and her face was no longer *sad.* Then they arose early in the morning and worshiped before the LORD, and returned again to their house in Ramah. And Elkanah had relations with Hannah his wife, and the LORD remembered her. It came about in due time, after Hannah had conceived, that she gave birth to a son; and she named him Samuel, *saying,* "Because I have asked him of the LORD."

1 Samuel 1:1–20

Hope

Because we are talking about prayer again in this chapter, I'd like to first and foremost say a few words about Shiloh. Shiloh is the place where Hannah took the desperation she had in wanting a son to the One who was more than capable of opening her womb. Shiloh is where the tent of meeting was pitched. The tent of *meeting.*

Shiloh is your prayer closet. Shiloh is the place where you meet with Him. Shiloh is where you take the desperation of your heart to the One who can answer it. Shiloh is the place where you cast your anxieties on Him and bring your supplications and petitions before Him. And Shiloh is the place where *hope* is never forfeited and where hope stays alive.

There are few things in this life that we can't live without. You can't live without food. It's called starvation. You can't live without water. It's called dehydration. And you can't live without hope.

Think about it.

When you have nothing to live for, what's the point of living? People die when they give up. They die internally, shriveling up inside, and they can die externally. People have succumbed to sicknesses and diseases as a result of a lack of hope and people have taken their own lives due to its absence as well. Some people, it's rumored to believe, have actually died as the result of a broken heart—a heart without hope.

Proverbs 13:12 says that hope deferred makes the heart sick. Our hearts become sick when we put our hope in anything and in anyone other than Christ. He's the answer. He's the source of all life. It's who He is that allows us to have hope in the first place. He's faithful and good. His word does not return void. (See Isaiah 55:11.) And He's prepared a place for me. (See John 14:2.) So many people, however, have given up and lost hope in the midst of whatever it was they were waiting for.

Singer and songwriter, Tom Petty, once said this in his song "The Waiting:"[1] "The waiting is the hardest part." It's *the waiting* that gradually seeks to squeeze hope out of the heart. Indeed, the heart doesn't lose hope instantly. It can be a slow, agonizing death. When the realities of our circumstances have a louder voice than the promises of God, we lose hope. Our vision becomes cloudy, hazed over by what we are going through, until we are completely blinded by what *appears* to be impossible or never ending.

The truth is that we can either be defined by the waiting or by the promise. In all honesty, it's never about *the waiting*. It's about the *One* who promised. He's unchanging. When Paul described the afflictions he was going through as momentary (see 2 Corinthians 4:17), he was essentially saying that his persecutions and hardships would only last for a moment. They were subject to change. They did not compare to what was waiting for him in heaven—an eternal weight of glory. Eternity is forever. This life and what we go through is temporal. Paul understood this. He lived his life for eternity. When you have a vision of something that's larger than yourself and what you are going through, you can go through anything. Your hope doesn't run out because your hope is in what's waiting for you, *the promise*, not what's happening around you. It was for the joy set before Jesus that He endured the cross. (See Hebrews 12:2). His joy was not in the sufferings of the cross. His joy was in what the suffering was going to yield. His joy was in what was on the other side of the cross, a family reunion of lost sons and daughters.

My college friend and roommate, Craig Austin, played football for Millersville University. He was the starting full back for the Marauders. He was a big guy! He could bench 405 lbs. two times! That may not mean a whole lot to you, but it's a big deal to a guy like me who has spent a lot of years lifting weights! Not only was Craig a bruiser on the field, he was also extremely bright. He majored in botany and minored in biochemistry while at Millersville. He later went on and received his PhD from Cornell University.

While living together, I questioned Craig one day about all the training he was doing in the off season for the football team. He would often have to be up early enough to run with the team by 5:00 a.m.! I wasn't trying to be a Debbie Downer or pessimistic. I just knew that no one from Millersville ever went on to play in the NFL. I just couldn't understand why anyone would put themselves through what he was putting himself through without any long term payoff. Why go through all of those practices and early mornings when you know you aren't going to make it to the big show?

This is the education I received from him one day when he said, "When Saturday comes, it makes it all worth it." Saturday was game day. Saturday was the joy set before him. This is what Craig was ultimately saying: "It doesn't matter what I go through or subject myself to. None of that compares to the thrill of playing in the game." What an awesome perspective. There were a lot of practices, a lot of time spent in the weight room and a lot of time studying and memorizing not only his own team's play book but also game footage from other teams. There were a lot of early mornings and injuries. There were years and years of playing from Pee Wee Football to high school varsity. And there was a lot of preparation and waiting to achieve what he did to become the starting full back for our beloved alma mater. But it was all worth it when Saturday came.

Year after Year

The Bible is loaded with examples of people who had to wait a long time before they received the fulfillment of their hope or what was promised to them. Abraham and Sarah waited *twenty five years* until their promised son, Isaac, was born. Jacob waited *fourteen years* before he was able to finally marry Rachael. Israel spent *forty years* wandering around in the wilderness before finally laying hold of the land promised to them and *seventy years* in Babylonian captivity before their release.

That's a long time! Again, we can't be too quick to miss what those years of waiting must have felt like. They really happened! Put yourself in their shoes. Read the Bible with feeling! In the Gospels, Jesus encountered a woman who had been bent double by an evil spirit for eighteen years and another woman who had a hemorrhage for twelve years before healing them. He also ran into a man who had been ill for thirty-eight years at a pool in Jerusalem called Bethesda. As I had already mentioned before, nothing is written in the Bible in an effort to fill space. Every word counts. Every word is significant. Those years of waiting are included for a reason. Why? Because we can all relate in our own way. We've all had to wait for things and our faith was challenged and stretched in the midst of it.

Thirty-eight years is a long time for you to believe things about yourself that aren't true that your circumstances seem to imply. In fact, your identity can be shaped and molded by the fact that you have been ill for that long. Thirty-eight years is a long time to maintain and not let go of hope. This is why Jesus asks the man if he wants to get well. (See John 5:6.)

This man had spent many years trying to get into the pool when the angel of the Lord went down at certain seasons to stir up the water. Whoever was able to get into the pool first after the water was stirred would be instantly healed. Thirty-eight years is a long time to wait... Thirty-eight years is a long time to watch person after person beat you to your answer. Thirty-eight years is a long time to be conformed to the disease that's afflicting you.

Jesus asked if the man wished to get well because frankly there aren't a whole lot of people who do wish to get well. To become well requires responsibility. You can no longer justify your actions based on what you've gone through or what's been done to you. All too often, whatever has assailed someone has become a part of who they are. They wouldn't know who they were if they were to live free of their sickness, disease, or affliction. We can even take it a step further and say that there are some people who don't want to let go of the anger, bitterness, unforgiveness, and judgments they hold toward certain people because they wouldn't know who they are without them. It's been their story for so long. It's been the script they've acted out over and over again. The lines are memorized. It's a role they've lived for years and all the while Jesus comes to us with a better story, a better script, and a better role. All we have to do is let go of the very thing that's killing us. All we have to do is give to others what He has freely given to us.

We don't have to be pottered by the waiting, guys. We can be clay that's molded by hope and faith and placed within the fire of His love. Romans 5:5 tells us that hope doesn't disappoint because the love of God has been poured out in our hearts through the Holy Spirit. Hope is the byproduct of His love. It's totally legal to have hope as a Christian because of His love. His love assures us that He's faithful and that He provides and cares for His children. His love is what sent His Son in the first place.

(See John 3:16.) I can have hope because my hope is in His love, and as long as it remains there, I will never be disappointed. In fact, Jesus encouraged us to make our home in His love, to abide there. (See John 15:9.)

My children know that I love them. Because this is a reality in their lives, they come before me with confidence and boldness and ask me for whatever their heart desires. They know I'll come through for them because they know my heart. They aren't afraid of being punished. They know I have the ability to grant their request. They have hope and they have courage.

Likewise, Hebrews 4:16 encourages us to draw near to the *throne of grace* with confidence. Don't you just love that *that's* the title of God's throne? In the book of Esther, no one was allowed to come before the king in the inner court unless they were summoned and unless the king extended the golden scepter to them. (See Esther 4:11.) In Hebrews 1:8, we read that Jesus's throne is forever and ever and that the righteous scepter is the scepter of His kingdom. I want you to know that *that* scepter has been extended toward you. His blood has made you righteous. You stand completely right before Him and as a result, you can come before Him. You are always summoned. You are always welcome.

For nearly two years, my oldest daughter, Emma, would barge into my bedroom every morning with the same demand—"I want my gummies (vitamins) and chocolate milk." Day after day, the same words would be uttered. Sometimes, she waltzed in before the sun had a chance to wake up! The more she exercised her right as my daughter to come into my room in the manner she did, the more God began to speak to me through her example. He showed me that Emma came into my bedroom with boldness because she knew she wasn't going to get a good tongue lashing. It never crossed her little mind that Daddy was going to punish her for waking him out of his sleep. Her confidence came from the fact that she knew I loved her. She knew I would respond.

She was perfected in my love and perfect love casts out all—*fear*. (See 1 John 4:18.)

In the same way that my children come boldly before me, Hannah came boldly before the Lord. She didn't come into His presence with her petition for a son once or twice. She did it many times. In 1 Samuel 1:7, we read the words *year after year*. Year after year, Elkanah, Hannah's husband, would leave his city to go to Shiloh to worship and sacrifice to the Lord. Year after year as Elkanah's family went up to the house of the Lord, Peninnah, Elkanah's second wife and Hannah's rival, would provoke Hannah by pointing out that she had children but Hannah did not. Every year that passed was the constant reminder of what Hannah didn't have and what her heart cried out for. And year after year, she sought the Lord for it.

While Elkanah was worshiping and sacrificing and while Peninnah ridiculed and antagonized, Hannah was praying. In the face of barrenness, in the face of her rival's taunts, in the face of the years of waiting, Hannah never lost hope. Her desperation grew larger with every passing year and because nothing or no one else could be the answer to her desperation, she *needed* God to open her womb. The One who closed it was also the One who could open it. It's one thing to be desperate and to have a groaning inside of you that's too deep for words, but it's another thing to know where to take it.

Again, Hebrews 11:1 tells us that faith is the *assurance* of things *hoped for*, the conviction of things not seen. Hannah had an assurance to her hope. If she didn't, she wouldn't have been praying. Even through tear-stained cheeks and an empty stomach that refused to eat, she never lost hope. Why? Because God was her assurance.

She wasn't defined by the waiting. She was defined by the One who met her in Shiloh. She had faith in His ability. There was nothing that Elkanah could do for her even though he may have been better to her than ten sons. (See 1 Samuel 1:8.) Her desperation required the intervention of God.

Tears of Distress and Silent Lips

In chapter 7, I explained that the Hebrew word for *meditates* is translated as "to moan or groan, growl, utter, speak, muse." In 1 Samuel 1:10, it says that Hannah was greatly distressed and that she prayed to the Lord and wept bitterly. The words *wept bitterly* in this verse are translated from the Hebrew word *bakah*, and it means to weep or bewail. Bewailing is a lot like growling and groaning. In 1 Samuel 1:12–13, it says that Eli the priest was watching Hannah pray and that he noticed that although her mouth was moving, her voice was not heard. She was speaking in her heart. She uttered in silence.

Hannah's prayers are a great example of what it looks like for desperation to be expressed through meditation and watching and praying. She knew God could open her womb, and she meditated on and waited upon that fact but that doesn't mean that she didn't *feel*. Her tears were very real. She was oppressed in spirit and she was bitter. Have you ever felt that way? Have you ever heard that voice that would say things such as the following in the midst of waiting?

- "Well, if it was going to happen it would have happened by now."
- "Look, let's face it; you're not getting any younger."
- "Are you sure you heard God say that?"
- "Why waste your time?"
- "Why would He want to do that for you?"
- "What makes you think you're so special?"
- "You've been praying for so long and it hasn't made a difference yet."

That's the voice of Peninnah. That's the voice of your rival, the thief of hope and faith. That's the enemy trying to rob you of your destiny. That's Goliath laughing in David's face.

Could you imagine the voices that must have infiltrated Hannah's thinking?

- "You're not good enough"
- "There's something wrong with you."
- "You can't provide."

- "Peninnah is a far better wife than you. At least she could conceive."
- "You're under a curse."
- "It'll always be this way."

Every time she glanced at Peninnah's children, she was continuously reminded of what she lacked. Even though she was conscious of what she didn't have, she was more conscious of the One who could help her. The tears from her bitter weeping were real. The groaning was real. But her faith was even more real.

As I had already mentioned in chapter 4, I do not believe that Hannah's desire for a son was birthed as a result of jealousy toward Peninnah. She desired a son because it was God's plan for her life. He brought Israel's first prophet, Samuel, through a *desperate woman*. The desire for a son was conceived and fulfilled in Shiloh in the tent of meeting, in the secret place. It was there that she cried out. It was there that she was heard.

It was in Shiloh where her desperation rang out with the echoes of her weeping and groaning. In fact, it's the groaning that prepares you for what's coming. Every woman in labor groans and pushes until her baby is born. It's a part of the delivery process. Similarly, the groaning from within yourself reveals what it is that God wants to do in your life.

What are you groaning for? What are you desperate for? Has your desperation translated over to necessity? What do you need God to do in your life? What are you waiting for? Can you walk through the "year after years" of life and not give up? Are you willing to return to Shiloh for however long it takes? What if it's twenty-five years like it was for Abraham and Sarah? What if it's fourteen years like it was for Jacob? How desperate are you?

Hannah's desperation led her to fast while praying. Food couldn't satisfy her. Her hunger could only be satiated by the answer to her petition. We don't fast to bend God's arm and make Him do what we want. We fast because we are hungry. We fast because we are desperate. We want to be filled with our heart's desire. We fast to draw near to Him. If you are interested in learning more about fasting, I highly recommend Mahesh Chavda's book entitled *The Hidden Power of Prayer and Fasting: Releasing the Awesome Power of the Praying Church.*

Yes and Amen

While Eli was watching Hannah pray, he concluded that she was drunk. (See 1 Samuel 1:13.) I'm going to tell you something right now. The more desperate you are, the crazier you are going to appear to others. They will not understand your pursuit, but please do not let that deter you. The last thing you need to do is calm down. Keep going. Hunger and thirst is the sign that you are *awake*. You're not playing games. You want what's been promised to you. And the thing I desire the most above everything else is this promise: "He who did not spare His own Son, but delivered Him over for us all, how will He not also with Him freely give us all things?" (Rom. 8:32).

Many people read this verse and believe that the words *freely give us all things* is a reference to getting anything and everything under the sun. If God didn't spare His own Son, won't He freely give me whatever I want? That is not what this verse is implying when read in light of the context it was written in. It's written in the context of becoming like Jesus. Here it is in its proper framework:

> For those whom He foreknew, He also predestined *to become conformed to the image of His Son, so that He would be the firstborn among many brethren*; and these whom He predestined, He also called; and these whom He called, He also justified; and these whom He justified, He also glorified. What then shall we say to these things? If God *is* for us, who *is* against us? He who did not spare His own

Son, but delivered Him over for us all, how will He not also with Him freely give us all things? (emphasis mine).

Romans 8:29–32

Freely give us all things was written in reference to God giving to us all that's required to accomplish what's written in verse 29, to be conformed to the image of His Son. These *things* are what my heart desires. I want to be just like Him and I realize that I can't do it on my own. I *need* Him to do it. My desperation has met necessity. Like Hannah, I seek Him in secret in my *Shiloh*, knowing full well that if He predestined me to be conformed to the image of His Son, He will freely give to me all that's required to make that my reality. Second Corinthians 1:20 tells us that as many as are the promises of God, in Him (Christ) they are yes; therefore also through Him is our Amen to the glory of God through us. In other words, if God promised it, it's a yes through Christ and we say amen because we agree. As a result, God is glorified by His promises coming to pass in our lives.

The Greatest Prayer Ever Prayed

Hannah wanted a son to be conceived within her womb, and she promised that if God gave a son to her, she would give him to the Lord all the days of his life. (See 1 Samuel 1:11.) God answered her prayer. In 1 Samuel 1:17, we read that Hannah received the blessing of Eli the priest, and in 1 Samuel 1:19, we read that Elkanah had relations with his wife, Hannah, and that the Lord remembered her. The word *remembered* can also be translated to say that the Lord went into action on her behalf. He gave her a son. He gave her a prophet. And Hannah would go on to keep her promise and God would be glorified through it.

Hannah gave back what was conceived. Something has been conceived within me as well. First Peter 1:23 mentions that I have been born again by His imperishable seed. My whole life I was looking for the One who never stopped loving me and

210

the One who could save me. I was desperately searching in all the wrong places, but all the while He knew who I was looking for. He answered my desperation that one night in my mother's living room at nineteen years of age. He heard the cry of my heart when I didn't know how to verbalize it. He interpreted my groaning and He answered. He found the one who was lost and He saved him. In the same way that the Holy Spirit planted Jesus inside of Mary's womb, He's been planted in me as well and just like Hannah gave Samuel to the Lord, I've given myself to Him.

On July 26, 2011 God had awakened me from my sleep and said, "Brian, if the church would learn to pray like my Son, the world would look completely different." At first, I thought he was talking about what we commonly refer to as the "Lord's Prayer" found in Matthew 6:9–13 or maybe what we also refer to as the "High Priestly Prayer" found in John 17. But I quickly discovered that those prayers that Jesus prayed were not what He had in mind. He was referring to Jesus's prayer found in John 12:28 where Jesus prayed these four simple words: "Father, glorify Your name." Jesus was ultimately saying that it wasn't about Him (although it is all about Him). He wasn't on the earth to make a name for Himself (although He was given the name above every other name). He wasn't seeking to be saved from the hour of His suffering. He *gave* Himself to the will of His father. Because I desperately want the Father to be glorified in my life, I also give myself to His will for me.

Be Persistent

The desperation to *believe* the gospel has also been conceived within me. I'm desperate to understand what the woman with the alabaster vial, the woman at the well, and the woman caught in adultery understood. I'm desperate to love the way He loves and to be just like Him. These things have been conceived within me and they are growing. Like Hannah, I need Him to remember me. I need Him to go into action on my behalf. I couldn't save myself and I can't make myself be like Him. Even if I have to wait year after year, so be it. It's not about the waiting. It's about the promise.

Like Hannah, there is nothing that this world could offer that can scratch my itch. Only He can do for me what I desire. Elkanah couldn't grant Hannah's request. He couldn't quench her thirst. But God could *and* did. I don't know what else to do but to do what Hannah did. I seek Him. I meditate. I watch and pray. And yet I do all of this without losing hope. I'm coming to Him in faith.

In Luke 18:1–8 Jesus shares a parable about an unrighteous judge and a widow illustrating to His disciples that *at all times they ought to pray and not lose heart.* (See Luke 18:1.) Why? Because the waiting wants your heart to fail. The waiting seeks to bleed your heart dry and Jesus is telling us through this parable that prayer is the one thing that protects your heart from dying. It's a safeguard. The widow in this parable kept coming before the unrighteous judge to cry out for legal protection from her opponent. Wearied by her constant nagging, the unrighteous judge grants her request. This is what Jesus said after He finished telling the parable: "Hear what the unrighteous judge said." (See Luke 18:6.)

What did the unrighteous judge say? "Even though I do not fear God nor respect man, yet because this widow bothers me, I will give her legal protection, otherwise by continually coming she will wear me out" (Luke 18:4–5).

Don't stop seeking. Don't stop asking. Don't stop knocking. The fact that you do such things is the evidence that you have faith. You believe He will reward you. Hannah believed that as well. That's why she never stopped.

Prayer is the only thing that I know how to do anymore. In my desperation, I meditate on who He is and what He wants to do and watch and wait for it to become my reality. Some of us have been waiting for things for a long time. You might be waiting for circumstances to change. You might be waiting to be healed. You might be waiting for finances to come in. Whatever you are waiting for, it can feel like a time of barrenness. Be like Hannah. Be like the widow in Luke 18. Bring your desperation before the One who hears you and remember that the desire of your heart is the byproduct of what He wants to do in your life.

For me, I want to believe. I need God to do a deeper work in my own heart. I can't simply walk by people anymore. I want to interrupt Walmart shoppers by shouting, "I have an announcement" and share the Gospel with them. If it's really real, guys, shouldn't our hearts burn? Shouldn't we be overtaken by the kindness and forgiveness shown toward the three women in this book? Shouldn't we stop wearing the clothes of a dead man and act as if we are alive? The Gospel is the best thing that has ever happened to us. It must become our reality.

No more games.

It's time to see. It's time to believe.

Father, I pray that what the reader has read in this book will become a reality in his or her life. Open our eyes, God. Open our hearts. Do a deeper work within us. We need You, God. We can't do this without You. We can't read about love and then go do it. Help us to become it. Make every motive within us to flow out of the pure place of love. I pray that you would crush fear in our lives and cause boldness to rise up. O that we would seek you, God. O that we would pray. We give ourselves to you believing that you will finish the work you started within us. Bring it to pass. Make us to believe. Make us to see. Make the beauty of this gospel real in our lives.

Epilogue

Dusty Road
by Michael Ketterer[1]

And I've been gone for
a long time now,
a wanderer on this dusty road.
And I'm crying out, I'm
crying out for you God,
to come to me, and
lead me home.

I'm ready now. I've
changed my heart.
I'm running into, into your arms.

And you meet me Father
on this dusty road.
And you come with a ring,
and you come with a robe.
And you meet me Father
on this dusty road.
And you wipe away my tears,
and you lead me home.

And I believe, Oh I believe…
that you love me God,
that you want me God

There's so much in those words. A wearied wanderer falls into the loving arms of a father who has been waiting for his return. While one was out searching, the other was left waiting. When one's search ended, the other's began as he looked down the road in hopes that his son would crest the horizon. We've walked that dusty road, and we've felt the warmth of our Father's embrace. It's our story. But it's a story we must believe.

He came to seek and save the lost. He came to seek and save you and me. It's the greatest love story ever told. The Creator of the universe never waited to scold you. He waited to hold you. He didn't wait to punish you. He waited to love you. He didn't say, "I told you so." He clothed you. He didn't come to divorce you. He came to marry you. His life was the courtship. His death was the proposal. All anyone needs to say is yes.

We have to get it. We need to be able to say with confidence, "I believe, oh I believe that you love me God, that You want me God." Because it's true. Let's unite what we have heard with faith. Let's wipe the dust of our past off of our feet and understand that we're home. He's brought us back into the fold. We've been adopted. We belong to Him. His story is our story. Let's live it out. May our lives be the letters on the pages. Let's make history together.

Before this book comes to a close, let's take a look at the lyrics to one more song because they are worth meditating on. Indeed, they must become a reality in our life. We must see. We must believe. We must come awake! May they be to you a source of exhortation and encouragement.

Christ is Risen
by Matt Maher[2]

Let no one caught in sin remain
inside the lie of inward shame
We fix our eyes upon the cross
And run to him who
showed great love
And bled for us
Freely You bled, for us

Christ is risen from the dead
Trampling over death by death
Come awake, come awake!
Come and rise up
from the grave!

Christ is risen from the dead
We are one with him again
Come awake, come awake!
Come and rise up from the grave

Beneath the weight of all our sin
You bow to none but heavens will
No scheme of hell, no
scoffer's crown
No burden great can
hold you down
In strength you reign
Forever let your church proclaim

Christ is risen from the dead
Trampling over death by death
Come awake, come awake!
Come and rise up from the grave

Christ is risen from the dead
We are one with him again
Come awake, come awake!
Come and rise up from the grave

Oh death! Where is your sting?
Oh hell! Where is your victory?
Oh Church! Come
stand in the light!
The glory of God has
defeated the night!

Oh death! Where is your sting?
Oh hell! Where is your victory?
Oh Church! Come
stand in the light!
Our God is not dead,
he's alive! he's alive!

Christ is risen from the dead
Trampling over death by death
Come awake, come awake!
Come and rise up from the grave
Christ is risen from the dead
We are one with him again
Come awake, come awake!
Come and rise up from the grave

Rise up from the grave...

We will rise up from the grave when we understand what it is that Matt has written through these lyrics. Let's fix our eyes on the cross. Let's understand that He freely bled for us. Let's come to the knowledge that we are one with Him again. Let us come awake! The glory of God has defeated the night! Hallelujah!

Notes

Prologue

1. Lyrics from the song "Fall Afresh" by Jeremy Riddle from the album *Furious*.
2. Lyrics from the song "I Still Haven't Found What I'm Looking For" by U2 from the album *The Joshua Tree*.

Introduction

1. For more information on Joyce Meyer and her ministry, visit her website: http://www.joycemeyer.org/.
2. Philip Yancey (1997). *What's So Amazing About Grace?* Grand Rapids, MI: Zondervan. Pg. 11.
3. This is an excerpt Nic Billman's sermon at the end of the extended version of Nic and Rachael Billman's song "The Invitation" from the album *In the Sound of Your Heartbeat*.

Who's Looking for Whom?

1. For more information on Rick Pino and his ministry and music, visit his website: http://www.rickpino.com/.

Tears, Perfume, and Feet

1. Lyrics from the song "Alabaster Box" by Cece Winans from the album *Alabaster Box*.
2. Here is the website where I had found the information cited concerning dragonflies and their meaning: http://www.dragonfly-site.com/meaning-symbolize.html.

H_2O

1. Lyrics from the song "Sweep Me Away" by Nic and Rachael Billman from the album *In the Sound of Your Heartbeat*.
2. For more information about Steffany Frizzell Gretzinger and her music, visit her website: http://www.bethelmusic.com/artist/steffany-frizzell-gretzinger.

The Okay Corral of the Gospel

1. Lyrics from the song "I Am Hephzibah" by Julie Meyer from the album *God Is Alive*.
2. For more information on Bill Johnson and his ministry, visit his website: http://bjm.org/.

You Can Have It Too

1. Quotes about prayer by Leonard Ravenhill were taken from the following sources:

   - http://www.truthsource.net/quotes/?q_sort=authors_list&sort_author=Leonard_Ravenhill.
   - http://www.goodreads.com/author/quotes/159020.Leonard_Ravenhill
   - http://www.leonard-ravenhill.com/category/excerpts

2. For more information on the deceased Leonard Ravenhill and his ministry and the impact it had on upon the history of Christianity, visit his website: http://www.ravenhill.org/.

The Secret Place

1. To read this article in its entirety, please visit the following website: http://www.ravenhill.org/prayer.htm. Copyright (C) 1994 by Leonard Ravenhill, Lindale, Texas.

Desperation

1. Lyrics from the song "The Waiting" by Tom Petty from the album *Hard Promises*.

Epilogue

1. Lyrics from the song "Dusty Road" by Michael Ketterer from the album *Love/War/Solar System*.
2. Lyrics from the song "Christ is Risen" by Matt Maher from the album *Alive Again*.